All Exclusive

By Hugh Morrison

ISBN-13: 978-1502786234

© Hugh Morrison 2014. All rights reserved.

Published by Montpelier Publishing, London. Printed by Amazon Createspace. All characters appearing in this work are fictitious. Any resemblance to real persons, living or dead, is purely coincidental.

Author's note: This novel is based on the play of the same name, published by Lazy Bee Scripts. It was first performed at the Sean O'Casey Theatre, Dublin, in May 2013.

To the memory of
Keith Waterhouse CBE
1929-2009

Prologue

Excerpt from the website of the San Itairi Ministry of Tourism (*Minesterio de Comercio y Turismo de San Itairi*):

You are Welcome in San Itairi! This tiny island of the Caribbean, known as the 'Little Sister of Cuba' is waiting to capture you with its warm embrace of beaches, food and culture. Here there are regular flights from the UK and Germany, and you can stay at the top quality Las Cantatas hotel complex which features modern western standards of accommodation. Wander in the cobbled streets of the Old Town, or in the pretty wooded hills outside the town (restricted access only). Columbus, the famous explorer, said that the island was so beautiful that he must not stay but leave it 'only to God'. We are sure you will never want to leave!

Excerpt from the *Radical Planet Guide to the Caribbean:*

There is not a great deal worth stopping for on the little island of San Itairi. Columbus famously didn't want to stay, and if you make the trip you'll probably understand why. This rocky, wooded outcrop, just 18 miles wide by 27 miles long, is a gruellingly rough four hour ferry ride from Havana, or if you're very brave you can make the trip from Cuba by light aircraft.

One of the island's few claims to fame is that it is the home of Miguel Corantes, the conceptual artist, who caused controversy when his installation *Take Me I'm Whores,* comprising two tons of manure, was on display briefly in London's Tate Modern gallery (and later had to be removed for health and safety reasons). The island's right wing authoritarian government under Felipe

Rivera, who seized power in a coup in 1989 (rumoured to have been bankrolled by the CIA), have ensured however that none of Corantes' works are on public display. What could have been a source of revenue and cultural tourism has therefore been lost, and the Old Town's two galleries now contain little more than bland figurative art acceptable to the government and the church.

There are rumours however that the ageing Rivera is losing his grip and calls for a democratic government are increasing. In a bid to modernise and bring in tourism, in 2003 the airstrip was widened to allow direct charter flights from the UK and Germany. The large, all-inclusive Las Cantatas holiday complex was built near the Old Town (taking over the island's only beach in the process). This, the island's only large hotel, is run by the UK Solarflair leisure group. Beware – it caters for the worst aspects of the British and German package holiday markets. Full English breakfasts, bingo and karaoke are some of the delights on offer, and the streets of the Old Town are now infested by groups of drunken holidaymakers on 'wine tasting' tours and the like. If despite all this you would still like to visit, you are advised to go in low season (November-March) and not to stay the night.

 Wifi access rating: poor
 Disabled facilities rating: poor
 Gay and lesbian friendly rating: nil

Reviews from Travel Advisor.co.uk website:

'Dont bother'

By Reg and Jean Brooks, Beckenham.

We stay'd at the "Hotel" Cantasas dont bother it is noisy, food is terible.Rooms not clean and when we asked for another just got a shrug and told to Complain in UK. "Day Trips" were expesive not worth the effort as theres nothing to see on the Island. Flight is too long, 12 hours. Our "Rep" made an effort but you could tell her Heart was NOT in it. We wont be going back next year.

'Terrible'

By Cheryl and David Walters, Ipswich.

We stayed at Las Cantatas on a last minute deal to celebrate my husbands retirement. When we got there he wished he was still at work! Honestly we didnt realise place's like this existed anymore. Its like the worst type of Hotel from the Costa Brava, complete with "lager louts", non-stop noise and Football. We asked to be moved to another Hotel but were told, unbelievably, that it is the only one on the Island! We learned our lesson, pay a bit more and go somewhere select; we will be returning to Tenerife next year.

OMG you have 2go!!!

Lianne and Lisa Matthews, Doncaster

What can we say hotel cantatas is amazing!!! It as so much 2 do so little time the hotel is gr8 rooms a bit grunge but who cares your on holiday!! We done reps bar tour, banana boat, the food and drink was nonstop LOL big hello to rep Trisha, kids club manager and of course Kez and the Sheffield lads – gettem off!! CU next year!!!

One

Karen Kay made a final effort to get her suitcase closed by sitting on it. That always worked in films. There was an ominous cracking sound. Thinking she'd broken the catch or something, she jumped up and looked down at the case, only to find she'd been sitting on her sunglasses and had snapped them neatly in half. *Great start to the holiday*, she thought. The sunglasses cost a fortune and were supposed to make her look like Audrey Hepburn. *But now I'll have to mend them with sellotape.*

She couldn't imagine Audrey Hepburn going around Hollywood with taped-up glasses. *Actually, did they even have sellotape in the old days,* she wondered. She supposed she could always buy a cheap pair at the airport. *Who am I trying to kid anyway, thinking I look like Audrey Hepburn?* Audrey Hepburn with mousey hair, a big bum and a something dangerously approaching a muffin top round her waist. *Anyway, time to get cracking*, she thought....*hmm, bad choice of words....get* moving with the case.

She called out to Steve Trout, her boyfriend, who was already all packed and downstairs, looking out for the taxi.

'I'm nearly ready. Has it come yet?'

Her voice carried easily down the staircase of their two-bedroom starter home. The pokey rooms and paper-thin walls meant that shouted conversations could be carried out between them wherever they happened to be. Steve's parade ground voice, which he'd picked up in the army, boomed up the stairs.

'Can't see him. Said he was just round the corner when I called.'

Karen yelled back. 'They always say that! He'd better get a move on or we'll miss the flight! Why don't you call again?'

'What? What's the problem?'

She could tell he was getting annoyed. That was another thing she had noticed, that his temper was getting worse. He seemed to be suspicious and angry much more often since they'd moved in with each other.

'Never mind, I'm coming down'.

Karen started bumping her case down the stairs, the flimsy wood trembling with each impact.

'Mind that laminate, you'll scratch it'.

'Sorry. It's just a bit...could you help me?'

Steve tutted and walked up two of the stairs, took the case effortlessly in one hand, and plonked it down on the hall floor.

Karen felt like saying 'mind the laminate' but checked herself. That was at least something, she thought. Steve might not be much in the looks department, with his broken nose and sticky out ears that were made more obvious by his close-cropped hair, but he was certainly nicely built; not with that ape look that some muscular men have – as if they were carrying two invisible carpet rolls under their armpits – just, well...manly, like men used to be before they had gyms and steroids and waxing, like Sean Connery when he was young.

'Taxi's here' said Steve. 'He took his time'.

Steve picked up both their cases and flight bags and nudged the door open with his foot, trudging out into the tiny front garden. Karen felt a twinge of disappointment as she noticed what he'd finally decided to wear – his England football shirt, Adidas shorts, and black trainers. At least he wasn't wearing white socks (he'd finally got used to those little hidden ones that bought for him) but did he *have* to wear a football shirt and shorts - in October? She checked the snobbish thought and tried to tell herself she was just concerned about him catching cold.

The elderly asian taxi driver offered to help Steve but he waved him away and busied himself by stowing the cases into the boot of the little saloon.

Karen hurried out into the garden.

'Steve...won't you be cold? Why don't you wear your jeans?'

Steve straightened up and slammed the car boot shut, and walked round to the back door of the car to get in.

'Come off it babes, we're going on holiday. It'll be sweltering over there.'

'Yes, but it's a 12 hour flight first, and two hours' wait at the airport before.'

'Well I'm not going to freeze to death on a plane, am I?' He got into the car.

Karen sighed and went through her usual pre-holiday ritual of checking she'd done everything, in a kind of litany. Passport, yes, tickets, yes, plants yes, (stuck in the bath in two inches of water in the vague hope that one or two might survive the fortnight), money yes, door locked, yes – ready!

She got halfway down the path and had her usual obsessive-compulsive moment and went back to check if she'd actually locked the door, which of course she had.

As she slammed the door of the cab firmly shut (*can't be too careful in some of these old rustbuckets,* she thought) and inhaled the usual smell of stale cigarette smoke and air freshener, she suddenly realised she'd forgotten something.

'Wait, sorry, can you hang on?' she said as the driver began to put on his seatbelt.

'OK love, no problem' replied the driver, with an odd mix of Brummie and Indian accents.

'What is it now?' Steve said petulantly, crossing his arms.

'My book. I've forgotten my book.'

Steve rolled his eyes.

'That big one? We haven't got room for it. It weighs a ton.'

'It's not that heavy. I can fit it in my flight bag. It's a 12 hour flight, I'll need something to read.'

'Won't you be too busy trying to stop me freezing to death in my shorts?'

Karen didn't hear him as she rushed back to the house to find the book. Eventually she located it tucked under the IKEA coffee table, where she was sure she hadn't left it.

Triumphantly she grabbed it and raced back to the taxi, by now with its engine running and the driver drumming his fingers on the steering wheel. Karen jumped in and slammed the door firmly again, and the cab pulled out of their cul-de-sac.

The driver was chatty, and kept doing little half turns to look behind and talk to Karen and Steve. Karen mainly, as Steve had his arms crossed and was looking out of the window. He wasn't talkative at the best of times.

'So, going on holiday, is it?' asked the driver.

'That's right, for a couple of weeks'.

'Anywhere nice?'

Why did people always say 'anywhere nice' when asking about holidays, thought Karen. Did anyone ever actually reply 'no, we're going somewhere horrible?' Instead she smiled politely and said 'Yes, San Itairi'.

'Where?'

'San Itairi. Little island off Central America'.

'Oh, America. Nice place. My cousin lives there. Very good business in America'.

'No, not America, Central America, well, near it anyway.'

A white van overtook them a little too closely and the driver suddenly returned his concentration to the road.

'Cheers mate, nice passing, huh? Sorry love, you was saying?'

'I said it's near Central America. It's an island.'

'Oh, Ireland. You mean, Dublin, Cork, all those places, yes? My brother lives there, he says...'

He was cut off as a huge burst of static filled the car and then a crackly, incomprehensible voice squawked out from the two way radio. The car swerved as the driver fiddled with the mic and answered in some incomprehensible language.

Karen decided it was best to leave him to it. Actually she didn't know that much about where they were going anyway. The trip was a surprise from Steve, to celebrate their engagement, he said, and it was a last minute thing so it was pretty cheap, which was good as they were going to have to start saving for the wedding soon. She'd had a quick look at the hotel website and a couple of reviews, but that was it. As long as it was sunny and relaxing, that was all they needed right now.

As they sped along the dual carriageway on the last couple of miles to the airport, Karen had a sneaking suspicion that Steve had, perhaps not actually *hidden* her book, but put it somewhere conveniently out of sight. Another item for the little list of worries about her and Steve, she thought – the little list which seemed to be getting longer every day.

****

Ian Hurst staggered off the plane into bright early morning sunlight on the cracked tarmac of San Itairi Nuestre Senora airport. *Thank god that's over*, he thought. 12 hours on a flight that would put Easyjet to shame. And the people! Knocking back the free drinks as if there were no tomorrow, breaking into song from time to time, and even applauding when the plane finally touched down, as if they'd never seen a jet land before.

As editor of the Arts and Culture section on the *Daily Defender*, he had pulled off a near-miracle by managing to secure an interview with Miguel Corantes, the brilliant but reclusive conceptual artist. Miguel hadn't given an interview for four years and the government of San Itairi had refused him a visa to visit the UK, but the art world was buzzing over his latest piece in the Tate and Ian was sure that this exclusive interview would help revive the *Defender*'s flagging circulation.

The crowd of bedraggled holidaymakers, tetchy after the long flight, inched forward. In front of him was a barrel shaped man with a shaved head, the flesh on the back of his neck a pink roll partially covering a heavy gold chain, with a large blue vein across the glistening flesh. Looking closer, he realised that it wasn't a vein, but a tattoo in gothic script which read 'Villa Til I Die'. Ian shuddered and looked away.

An obese woman in a parallel queue on his left, squeezed into a small black sundress and displaying a prominent snake tattoo on her shoulder, dragged forward a painfully thin little girl, about ten years old, who was snivelling and rubbing her knuckles into her eyes. The woman shouted at her in a gravelly voice.

'I told you Lianne, you can't stay on the plane, now come on!'

The child continued snivelling.

'I wanted to watch that cartoon. It never finished.'

'Well you can't, we're going to the hotel. You can watch cartoons there.'

'Don't want to'.

The woman suddenly rapped the girl across the back of her head with her knuckles, but the girl barely flinched, as if used to it. Ian flinched too, and wondered if he should intervene in some way, then decided it was best not to get involved.

'Now don't you start. I've had just about enough of you for one day.'

The woman turned to look at Ian, her eyes lifted upward, as if to say, 'kids eh, what can you do with them?'

She must have noticed Ian's look of disgust. Her expression hardened and she looked him up and down with suspicion, then turned back to drag her daughter forward in the queue.

Ian suddenly felt distinctly overdressed in his tailored Oswald Boateng jacket, Vivien Westwood t-shirt, Armani jeans and Prada trainers. He held his laptop bag more tightly and looked around the shabby terminal building. A group of very young soldiers, conscripts, he supposed, were lounging against a wall, with rusty submachine guns slung over their shoulders. They were ogling a group of scantily clad, overweight girls in the queue, all wearing straw cowboy hats. The girls noticed they were being eyed up, and started giggling.

One of the girls stepped out of the queue and called out to the soldier.

'Hiya handsome, can I have a look at your weapon?' The group began cackling.

Some sort of airport guard or policemen, his slashed peak cap covering his eyes, then marched over angrily and began ushering the girl back into the queue. The group tutted and edged forward, looking at him with disdain.

'Alright Pedro, don't lose your rag', said one of them.

A ripple of laughter went through the queue, which moved forward as an official began stamping passports between puffs on a vile smelling cigarette.

Ian frowned. At least he only had to put up with this kind of thing at the airport. He pictured himself in a couple of hours or so, drinking something cool in Miguel's studio, where he'd been invited to stay the night. That would give him a chance to get refreshed before the dash back to London on the following day, when he'd have to go cattle class again. On previous foreign assignments, the *Defender* had sent him business class on BA, but now they'd fallen for all this austerity stuff. He recalled the conversation he'd had in his office a couple of days ago with Jane, the paper's admin manager who had arranged the travel for him.

'Bad news Ian, sorry but Finance have put a stop to all business class travel? It's strictly economy from now on?'

Jane was a tall, gangly blonde with big hipster glasses who had a habit of turning statements into questions, which even Ian found himself doing if he spoke for her for too long.

'I know that,' he replied. 'Bloody stupid if you ask me. Still, at least they haven't said I've got to interview him on Skype, so that's something. Economy in BA's not too bad I suppose.'

'Erm...actually there's a bit of a problem with that as well, Ian?'

'What do you mean, problem? BA flies to San Itairi, doesn't it? Or do I have to go by Virgin or something?'

'BA doesn't fly direct. You'd have to change at Kingston?'

Ian was momentarily confused. What did Kingston on Thames have to do with anything?

'Kingston?'

'Yes, Kingston, Jamaica? Then you'd have to fly to Havana with a stopover and then take a ferry? The whole trip takes 33 hours.'

'God almighty.'

He thought of his deadline. The article was supposed to appear in next week's culture section. If he wrote it on the plane he might just be able to do it, but it would be a tight squeeze.

'There's one other option though? Actually it's the only option because the BA flight goes over the budget limit as well as your carbon footprint allowance'.

Ian sighed. He'd forgotten the limits set on his travel weren't just financial. He twiddled with his i-phone.

'Tell me the worst'.

'I've managed to book you on a direct flight, it only takes 12 hours,' Jane replied brightly.

She's enjoying this, thought Ian. 'Great. From Heathrow I hope...?'

There was a pause. Ian's face fell. 'It's not Gatwick is it?'

Jane laughed. 'No, it's from South Midlands. It's a charter flight with a holiday company called Solarflair? So make sure you pack your sombrero!'

Ian didn't find it funny. He hadn't even heard of South Midlands airport or Solarflair. He decided however he wasn't going to give Jane the satisfaction of seeing him upset about it.

'Oh well, let's make the best of it then. Can you get me a car to this Midlands place?'

'Sorry Ian, no cars allowed now if trains are available. You're booked on the train from Euston. First class though, we got one of those special deals.'

'That's something anyway. Right, thanks Jane. I'll just have to remember to take my earplugs and blindfold.'

'Oh there's one more thing Ian. I know you're staying with Miguel but you'll never guess what, this Solarflair ticket comes with a holiday as well!'

Ian looked puzzled again. All this penny pinching seemed more complicated than it was worth.

'But I haven't got time for a holiday – I've got to get the article done right away and get back in time to talk about it on *Front Row*.'

'I know, what I mean is it's one of those package deals. You get a week's all inclusive accommodation in a hotel? The whole thing was actually the same price as the BA flight. You're supposed to stay for a week but they had an empty seat on the flight back the next day so I managed to get that for you instead? It took a bit of explaining, I can tell you.'

'Right, well that sounds lovely' replied Ian, sarcastically. 'I dread to think what the hotel will be like. What is 'all inclusive' anyway? Non-stop chips and drinks on tap or something?'

Jane laughed. 'Pretty much. If you go make sure you take your union jack swimming shorts.'

She laughed again and plonked the tickets on his desk.

Ian snapped back to the present as the passport queue finally moved forward and it was his turn to go through the gate. The guard scrutinised his battered passport and fingered the various visas and stamps on the pages. He asked something in Spanish, and then noticed Ian's blank look.

'You go holiday or business?'

'Business' replied Ian, firmly.

The obese woman in the other queue eyed Ian suspiciously as he hurried through the gate.

A few minutes later he was installed in a rusty taxi, bumping its way along San Itairi Town's shambolic ring road towards distant palm trees and Miguel's studio.

****

In the lounge of her immaculate semi, which appeared to be constructed mainly from white uPVC, Angie Belper had finally finished packing her two enormous suitcases. Years of experience of package holidays abroad had taught her to leave nothing to chance. She wanted to be sure she had everything she needed on holiday. A couple of outfits for each day, because she couldn't trust hotel laundries and she wasn't going to start washing things out at the sink when she was on holiday, plus all her usual bits and bobs.

She'd also had her hair done this morning at Fringe Benefits in the precinct; a nice jazzy looking shampoo and set and the roots touched up. The young girl in there who was always so perky had said it would take years off her, but Angie had put a stop to that by asking if she looked like she needed years taking off – the girl had gone quiet after that – always looking for a tip, that one was; well she didn't get one this time, that was for sure.

Angie's friend Pauline Beswick was coming with her, and so she'd come round in her old Fiat so she could leave it in Angie's drive for the fortnight. Angie wasn't too happy about that – it was a right grotty little thing and she hoped nobody in the Close would think it was hers; even though she didn't drive and they hadn't had a car since Harry had died, she'd rather have nothing at all on show than something shabby.

She looked at her jewel-encrusted watch (from the souk in Agadir; solid gold, so they said) squeezed on to her plump wrist, and, realising they had a bit of time left before they had to go, looked in on Pauline who was sitting in the conservatory. The gleaming uPVC structure, complete with three piece bamboo suite, was Angie's pride and joy, and had definitely added to the value of the house, as she always pointed out.

'Do you want a cup of tea before we go, Paul?'

'Oh yes please Ange, I'm parched.'

'Well get the kettle on then, you know where everything is'.

Angie sounded a little disappointed. 'Right you are then, Pauline. Having one yourself?'

'No thanks, I'm not risking the toilets at that airport. And use a mug, not those cups. They're for best'.

Pauline sighed. 'Yes, I remember from last time. Do you want a biscuit? I've bought some Rich Tea, I know you like to keep a good stock when you go abroad'.

Angie appeared in the conservatory, a little flustered.

'Honestly Pauline, I was up until midnight getting this place clean for when I'm away. I don't want crumbs everywhere. And we need to ration those biscuits over two weeks.'

Pauline bit her lip. 'Oh. So are you bringing quite a bit of food this time, like last year?'

'I told you I always do. You don't know what you'll get in these foreign places, so I've packed plenty of English stuff to keep us going in case. You know, pizzas, burgers, some Vesta curries, that kind of thing'.

Pauline remembered it was one of Angie's holiday rules to bring a lot of packaged food with her on holiday, not just biscuits. She was always worried about what the hygiene levels would be like. Most of them were quite good nowadays and cooked English food, but some still gave you funny stuff and you couldn't always tell what it was made of. She's already had to endure a long monologue from Angie about how she'd once found a sheep's eyeball staring out at her from a salad buffet that time in Hammamet.

Pauline decided against a biscuit and lit a ciggie instead. That was one thing at least about Angie, she didn't make a fuss about smoking in the house, well she couldn't really, as she was always smoking herself, but you had to do it in the conservatory with the window open. Though that was better than having to go out in the garden like most people had to these days, she thought.

'Right' said Angie. 'If you've made your tea, you drink that quick while I do the downstairs ensuite. I'd already cleaned it but you had to use it, so I'm giving it a quick once over with some Duck'. She disappeared into the tiny green lavatory under the stairs, brandishing a plastic bottle of lavatory cleaner.

Pauline sighed again and fingered her suitcase, which looked small in comparison with Angie's two huge wheeled monstrosities. She tried to interest herself in an article about Patsy Kensit's new diet in her copy of *Woman's Own*, but kept wondering, as she had been wondering these last couple of weeks, why she had agreed to go on holiday with Angie again.

When Pauline's husband Ron had died, Angie, who had never been a close friend, but a colleague at the bathroom superstore where they both worked, had taken her under her wing. To be honest she hadn't minded; she didn't have anyone else around since the kids had gone and mum was in a home, so she'd almost welcomed the attention.

Angie hadn't been so bad then; looking back Pauline suspected she got enough satisfaction browbeating poor old Harry at home and didn't have the energy to do it to anyone else.

A few weeks after Ron had gone, Harry died of a heart attack as well. Pauline had once heard a joke which went something like 'why do men usually die before their wives? Because they want to'. That joke was probably written for poor old Harry. Thereafter Angie was convinced they were bosom pals and had suggested they go on holiday. She was flush from Harry's life insurance payout, she said, and with her children in Australia (probably just living there to get away from her, Pauline thought), no-one else to ask. So they'd gone to Malta, to St Paul's Bay.

Pauline never really thought of herself as 'cultured' but she did like to see interesting places like churches and castles. She'd never really had the chance though. When she was 19 she was supposed to have gone to Khatmandu with some friends in a Bedford van, but they'd only got as far as Worksop when one of the wheels fell off and that was the end of it. Ron hadn't been into that sort of travel, and it turned out neither was Angie. Her preferred holiday activity seemed to be sitting around complaining.

Malta wasn't really her cup of tea – lots of youngsters and loud bars, that kind of thing, but it was alright, bright and cheerful and full of life and only a couple of hours on the plane. But Angie spent the whole time complaining about how dirty and common it was, and what was worse, seemed to blame *her* for everything.

Pauline was a forgiving sort, (too forgiving sometimes, Ron had said) and she'd forgotten the worst of the holiday. Eighteen months went by and Angie suggested a last minute autumn deal to some island place in the

Caribbean that was going cheap. If she was honest, she quite fancied a holiday; the summer weather had been awful, and the days without Ron seemed to hang heavily. She had no-one else to go with and in a fit of bravado mixed with self-pity, had agreed to it. So here she was; best put a brave face on it and make the best of it, she thought, as Angie bustled out of the ensuite with the sounds of a final flush and a reek of pine bleach in the air.

'Right, that'll pass muster, I think.' She consulted her watch again. 'Ten minutes 'til the taxi's here, though knowing that lot, they'll probably be late. Now, have you got everything? Passport, food, money?' I don't want you forgetting anything and us having to turn back.'

'No Angie, I've got everything. Oh, what did you say the name of the hotel was again?'

'Why do you need to know that?'

'Well...I just thought...if anything happens to us, if we get split up or something, I'll know where to go.'

'Pauline, how can we get split up on a plane? We're both 57 years old. We're going on holiday, not being evacuated. You don't need to have a luggage label round your neck. If anything goes wrong, just show your tickets to the reps and they'll sort it out'.

'But you've got my ticket, Angie'.

Angie sighed and rummaged in her handbag. She produced a computer printout carefully placed in a plastic holder.

'Oh for heaven's sake Pauline. Here, take your ticket then. Now, don't lose it.'

'Thanks Angie. I feel better knowing that'.

'Honestly I don't know what you'd do without me sometimes.'

Probably have a bit of peace and quiet on my own, Pauline was tempted to say, but then she heard the toot of a car horn outside. Angie began struggling with her two cases while trying to open the front door.

'Well give me a hand then – I can't do everything on my own!'

Pauline smiled feebly and began pulling her case and the larger of Angie's cases through the gleaming white uPVC door towards the waiting taxi.

'And don't get black marks on that door!'

Two

Ian wasn't comfortable with the way the interview was going. Partly it was jet lag, and partly the aftermath of the hot, dusty cab ride out to the remote studio, but he also got the feeling that he was the one being examined, and not in a good way either. In his interviews for the *Defender* and on the radio, men usually respectfully agreed with his views. They didn't try to have sex with him. That, however, was just what Miguel Corantes had tried to do, when halfway through the interview, he had leant over and ran his hand through Ian's hair and said he would like to go to bed with him.

Ian had stiffened (*at least not 'down there'*, he thought, grimly) and the look of shock on his face must have been obvious as Miguel had smiled and offered him a drink 'to help him relax'. He had now disappeared into the small kitchen off his studio and Ian could hear the sounds of bottles clinking.

It's not like I'm homophobic, thought Ian. *God, no* – but none of the many gay artists, writers and critics he was used to being around in London would have done anything as tacky as make a pass at an obviously straight guy. *Wasn't that kind of thing...well, didn't that go out in the 1970s?* Gay men were supposed to have 'gaydar' or something weren't they? Some instinctive way they knew other men were of the same persuasion before they made a move. Or was he just being reactionary? This was Latin America after all. Ian had already mentioned he had a partner – a female one – so surely Miguel must know he was barking up the wrong tree?

Ian pulled himself together as Miguel returned from the kitchen of his studio with two bottles of the local beer. Neither had been opened. Thank God, he thought, realising that meant nothing could have been slipped into them, then mentally slapped himself for even thinking Miguel would do something like that.

Miguel sat next to him on the sofa, not too close, thought Ian with relief, and deftly opened a beer and passed it to him. He clinked his bottle next to Ian's and smiled, his bushy black eyebrows raised quizzically.

'*Salud*'.

'Er...cheers...I mean, *salud*'.

Miguel raised the bottle to his lips, keeping his eyes on Ian.

Ian swallowed a gulp of beer and felt instantly better as the refreshing liquid poured down his throat.

'So. Don't worry. I see that you get nervous when I suggest we go to bed. It's ok. I see that you don't want.'

'No, no, I take it as a compliment, Miguel, don't get me wrong, I just...' Ian realised he was burbling. *This is pathetic*, he thought. *He's gay and made a pass at me. Nothing wrong with that. Get over it.*

'Is just what?'

Ian finally asserted himself, and sat up straight, imagining he was on *Question Time* and defending his viewpoint to some really reactionary Tory politician.

'It's just that I'm straight, Miguel. It's very flattering though'. He immediately wished he hadn't. *Next I'll be saying I always knew gay men had good taste*, he thought.

'Is OK. I have good taste, you know?'

Ian laughed weakly. Miguel laughed uproariously.

'But don't put that in your article, Ian.'

'Er...don't put what...?'

'That I am gay.'

Miguel took a long swig of his beer and gave Ian a dark look.

My god, thought Ian. *He's in the closet. Surely he's not trying to hide it? Then again...in this country, with a fascist government and in the grip of the Catholic church, who knows what he...*

Miguel laughed again.

'Ian, Ian. Gay, straight, lesbo, rental boy, these are all just labels! I am everything, a gay, a straight, a man, a woman...I am humanity. You know?'

This sounded a bit more comfortably abstract to Ian, though he wasn't sure where all this fitted in terms of gender politics. He suddenly wished his partner Jenny, a lecturer in Queer Theory at the University of Harlesden, were here to help.

'Er...so you're bisexual then?'

'Ha! Labels again. Ian. I am just sexual! When the mood takes me, I take the mood. You understand? Put that in your paper. Now, enough of this. Let me show you my new installation.'

The awkward moment seemed to have been smoothed over. Ian got up to walk over to the new installation, which took up considerable floor space in Miguel's already small, one room studio. It was a three dimensional collage of newspapers, all in Spanish, formed into a tortured shape about seven feet high, smeared with some kind of brown matter. Walking round the piece and scrutinising it, Ian felt back in control again; he imagined how he'd look on TV, presenting this on *London Tonight*'s cultural slot. He switched on the recorder on his i-phone.

Miguel suddenly spoke up. 'Is not shit'.

'Erm...no, no, of course it's definitely not shit. In fact it's incredible'.

'No, I mean, the brown on the papers. Is not shit. Is just paint.'

'Right. Does that choice of medium symbolise something?'

Miguel shrugged his shoulders. 'No, is just a hot country. More hygienic to use paint than real shit'.

'I see, that's intriguing.'

Ian took a swig of beer and continued his appraisal, his chin cupped in his palm.

'It's amazing. Gilbert and George made a big stir with this kind of thing'.

Miguel ran his hands through his bushy black hair in what seemed like anguish, and Ian wondered if he had done the wrong thing by comparing the work with other artists.

'Pah. Those two. They are out of touch, living a comfortable western life. This is about pain, Ian.' He raised his voice. 'About *reality.*'

This is incredible, thought Ian. *This is how it should be.* He'd always tried to relate art to the struggles of ordinary people around the world. Newspapers mixed with excrement; of course - it was all about misinformation. This was going to be one of the best articles of his career, he was convinced of it. He reminded himself that not only was he speaking to a leading conceptual artist, but also a major political voice in San Itairi's opposition movement, who the government might decide to lock up at any moment. Or worse.

Miguel interrupted his musings. 'Is not real shit but is meant to be. To symbolise state propaganda.'

Ian looked at the installation again. 'Of course, I see, yes. It really speaks about the situation right now in San Itairi'.

He'd tried to draw out Miguel's political activities without success. San Itairi, he remembered, had been a communist state from the early sixties, just after Cuba was liberated, until the fall of the Soviet Union, and dictator Felipe Rivera had been in power ever since. It was claimed he had CIA backing, but no-one had proved it. Every day, though, his corrupt grip on the country was growing weaker, and it was rumoured that a democratic socialist government, funded by foreign well-wishers, was organised and waiting to take over immediately when the time was right. He had a strong feeling that Miguel was involved in all this.

'True, true. Every day it gets worse. It is a good thing, Ian, you go back to London tomorrow. To a free country. To Europe.'

'I wouldn't say free, we have our problems too,' said Ian. He was about to tell Miguel about how he'd been part of a group calling for the resignation of an elderly reactionary art critic on a national newspaper, who had made insulting remarks about a Turner Prize winner, when he suddenly remembered he had been invited to stay the night. However, he'd accepted that before he knew the studio had only one room and that he would have to share it. He realised was going to hate himself for it, but he really didn't want to have to spend the whole night with one eye open for Miguel.

Ian swallowed and took a deep breath. 'Erm, yes, about staying over. Actually, plans have changed, the paper's asked me to do some coverage of events in San Itairi town while I'm here. Political stuff. So I'll be staying in a hotel in town. Sorry.'

Miguel looked crestfallen. Very much so in fact, which made Ian think he'd probably been right not to stay the night.

'Which hotel you stay in?' asked Miguel suspiciously.

Ian swallowed hard. Then he remembered the hotel booking that was part of the flight package. Las...Las...Christ, what was it called?

'Erm...Las something' said Ian weakly. 'But I can check the booking on here'. He raised his iphone.

'No need' replied Miguel, now looking less suspicious. 'It must be Las Cantatas. That is the only major hotel on the island anyway. Foreign owned. Exploiting the workers, who look after the pampered guests' every whim for food, and entertainment.'

'Sounds terrible. Still, that's what was booked for me, use it or lose, it, you know!' Ian waved the iphone again and wondered what that had to do with anything.

'It is the only hotel you could stay in anyway,' said Miguel. 'All the others, the little ones, are on strike.'

'On strike? That's awf...I mean, yes of course, I see – solidarity against the government. Good thing too.' Ian's hopes of finding a nice little authentic *pensione* suddenly disappeared.

Miguel took a step closer to Ian, who backed away slightly, freezing as he felt his back touch the installation.

'I am sorry you leave. We could have learnt much more from each other'.

'Yes, sure. But, well, it's not just your art that the world needs to know about. People need to know about the political problems here as well.'

Miguel nodded sadly. 'Yes, yes, you are right. You must go. Go, and tell the world of our problems.'

'Right then, I'll be off. If you could just call me a taxi, Miguel, that would be great. Not much Spanish I'm afraid.' Ian waved his iphone again in an increasingly desperate manner, laughed nervously and started to put his camera and laptop into his bag.

'Of course. I will telephone immediately. But before you go Ian, there is something I wish to show you. Something I think you will enjoy very, very much.'

Ian looked up from his case to see Miguel's bulk looming over him. Before he could say anything, Miguel took Ian's hand and began to lead him to a corner of the room. Outside, the cicadas began to chirrup as the sun reached its zenith.

****

Later that afternoon, Ian felt refreshed and back on form. What Miguel had shown him had revitalised him and made him realise just how important his article was going to be. The battered taxi bumped and swayed its way along the road from the wooded, secluded uplands where Miguel had his studio, down to the dusty plains surrounding the Old Town. He still felt rotten for turning down Miguel's offer of a bed for the night, but told himself that he'd only be able to assess the island's political situation accurately from the capital. Although he was principally an art critic and not a news reporter, art, after all, he thought, was inexplicably tied up with politics and so an article on art without some kind of political message would just be sentimental entertainment.

The taxi slowed as it reached heavy traffic on the main dual carriageway leading from the airport into the town. Ugly ribbon developments of concrete apartment blocks and white factories lined the road. The guide books were right that it wasn't worth visiting, he thought, then reminded himself that this wasn't just some paradise laid on for tourists, it was a real, working island; it wasn't there for his amusement. *Anyway*, he thought, *at least I won't have to worry about missing much when I fly back to London tomorrow*. He smiled to himself and felt his new energy running through his veins. He'd already seen the best thing in the country.

They passed a low building set in a palm-filled garden, and through the railings and with puzzled distaste Ian glimpsed a Union Jack fluttering from a flagpole. Below it two men were hurriedly packing bags into a white minivan. The taxi driver looked at him in the rear view mirror and nodded his head in the direction of the building.

'British Embassy. You British yes, or maybe German?'

'British' said Ian, folding his arms.

'Haha, very good. We like British and English here. Also Scottish. We not like German so much. British better.'

The taxi ground to a halt at the end of a long line of dusty cars. The driver muttered something in Spanish and fingered the crucifix dangling from the rear view mirror, then touched his fingers to his lips. Up ahead Ian could see a crowd of soldiers, policemen and bystanders milling around a car which had driven into a lamppost, with its windscreen shattered, partially blocking the road. Eventually a policeman in dark glasses started blowing a whistle and waving the traffic past.

They began to crawl along. Winding down the window to inhale a blast of hot air and traffic fumes, Ian saw a few feet away beside the car on the road, in a litter of debris, what was presumably a body under a red blanket. A paramedic and some sort of priest were kneeling beside it. The paramedic shook his head and the priest made the sign of the cross, followed by the policemen and soldiers. The driver did likewise.

Realising that the man on the ground was now a corpse, Ian's stomach lurched and he wondered what atheists were supposed to do in the presence of death. Bow? He could hardly bow in a car, and thought to himself that rituals surrounding death were just mumbo jumbo anyway, so he settled for taking a few pictures with his SLR instead, getting them done quickly before the man's face was covered. He suddenly realised he'd never seen a dead body before, not even one under a blanket.

One of the policemen noticed and strode over to the car. *Is he going to break my camera?* Ian wondered, with a tingle of adrenaline. If he could get a picture of that happening it would add to the article. Then he wondered how he would get a picture of it if his camera was broken. He'd have to juggle his iphone and it would all be a bit awkward.

The policeman ignored him and shook hands with the taxi driver; evidently they knew one another. After a brief and animated conversation the driver sped off as the angry sound of car horns from behind rose in volume. Ian wished he could understand Spanish, but the driver explained.

'Is big politician get killed. *Poof*, President no like him.'

Ian was confused. 'You mean he was killed for being a poof...er, I mean, for being gay?'

The driver looked at Ian in the rear view mirror with a puzzled expression. 'Gay? No, he not gay, he killed because he no good man. President's men shoot him.' He mimed a pistol being fired at his head and said 'poof' again, then blew imaginary smoke from his fingers.

'My god, you mean he was assassinated?'

'*Por favor*?' The driver looked puzzled.

Ian lapsed into the simplified pidgin English that he was used to using on trips abroad.

'Erm...president kill man?'

'*Si, si*, president kill him, he no good man, cause many trouble. Big communist.'

Ian was horrified. So an opposition politician had been killed? That was outrageous. He was definitely going to write about this, before the BBC or Reuters got wind of it. Perhaps this might even be the beginnings of San Itairi's Arab Spring? He took out his iphone and thrust it at the driver.

'So, do you mind if I ask you a few questions?'

Taking his eyes off the road for an alarmingly long time, the driver looked angry.

'You make record?'

'Recording, yes. I am a journalist'.

'Journalist? No understand.'

'Erm...reporter.'

'Ah, reporter! *Undante*. You write newspaper, yes?'

'Yes, from the *Daily Defender*.'

'Please?'

'From the BBC'. It was partly true anyway, he thought.

'Ah BBC, like Radio 2, yes? I hear on internet in hotel. Zoe Ball, Ken Bruce, very good music.'

Ian pursed his lips. 'That's the one. What do you think about the assassination?'

The driver turned back to the road and didn't speak. Ian thought for a moment that perhaps he hadn't understood. Then, cursing himself, he realised that the man was probably afraid to speak out against the government. He decided he would have to be more tactful.

'I said, I was wondering what you thought about the man who was killed. I won't need your name.'

The driver turned round and the car swerved briefly into the path of an oncoming moped. His face had gone red.

'My name Carlos Garcia and I tell you what I think. I think is good. That man, very big communist. Cause many troubles. President right to kill him. We no want communists back. Communism – finish!'

Ian frowned and clicked his recording app off. He noticed that behind the picture of a saint on the dashboard there was also a picture of Felipe Rivera in military uniform, looking uncannily like Colonel Gadaffi. He wondered if there was going to be an Arab Spring here after all. Besides, it was autumn now anyway.

The taxi lurched off the road into a long drive through a rubble-strewn field, which led up to what Ian assumed must be the Las Cantatas holiday complex. A row of white apartments with rust stains from their metal roofs lay at the end of the road, with a large white wall around it topped with what looked like broken glass. On the opposite side of the road a jeep was lurching towards them hooting its horn. As it passed Ian saw the back was full of scantily clad, heavily sunburnt tourists who shrieked at him as he passed, waving a bottle of tequila. The taxi driver smiled at Ian in the rear view mirror.

'This Hotel Cantatas. You have good time here. Many English people, always have good time!'

Ian started to wonder if he should have risked staying with Miguel after all.

Three

The cabin lights on flight SF108 from South Midlands to San Itairi dimmed and the passengers settled down as best they could to the long night ahead as the stewardesses cleared away the remains of the in-flight meal. Karen squirmed uncomfortably in the cramped window seat and realised that the back of her t-shirt was sticking to the plastic seat material. Steve was fiddling with the controls of the TV screen on the seat back in front of him. Fortunately the seat on Karen's left was empty so Steve had a bit more room to stretch out his long legs out of the way of the drinks trolley.

'Don't think it's working' he said in disgust.

Karen looked up from her book. 'I don't think any of them are working properly. I think they're only showing one film – everybody seems to be watching the same one.'

'What is it?'

Mall Cop 2, I think' replied Karen, without interest.

'Seen it. It was alright, don't think I'll bother again, though.'

'I think I'll read for a bit instead' said Karen, turning back to her book.

'That book again?' Steve wrinkled his nose. He wasn't much of a reader.

Karen looked up from the book and stared into middle distance, her mind drifting off into the twilight zone of long haul flying. She was pretty sure now that Steve *had* tried to hide her book. He hadn't minded her reading before, though he teased her about her growing collection of chick-lit novels with their brightly coloured covers and cartoony pictures of handbags and dresses, or women having romantic adventures in Paris or Milan. This book, however, seemed to annoy him. It was called *Beyond Art* and was full of wordy essays, which she found a bit slow going, but lots of pictures of conceptual art, abstract paintings and installations. She'd been recommended to read it as part of her evening class at the Worker's Educational Association.

Thinking back, things had started to go wrong when she'd signed up for that course. She'd thought at first that the tension between them was because of all the planning they were going to have to do for their wedding, but she realised that the problems predated Steve's uncharacteristically very romantic proposal when he took her for a surprise weekend away to Champney's health spa in Tring.

The WEA course was called 'Introduction to Art', and for two evenings a week Karen sat with a group of most elderly ladies, and one man, who she thought was probably gay, in a classroom in the adult education centre, while Fenella, their tutor, showed them slides of the great works of art of the past and talked about who painted them and what they all meant. She found it fascinating but a bit hard going. She'd been bright at school and got good 'A' levels. Mr Hall, her art teacher, who was really nice and encouraged her in her efforts at drawing, had suggested she should do an art foundation course at the local university, but mum and dad had talked her out of it – they said it wouldn't lead to anything and she would be better off getting a job straight away – but deep down Karen suspected that, like Steve did, they thought it was in some way 'getting above yourself'.

So she had got a good, if unexciting, administrative job at a local printing firm and had risen, through her twenties, to become Office Manager. That was how she met Steve; he had just come out of the army and was working in Goods In, meeting her daily to go over delivery schedules. The romance, as she supposed it must be, just sort of grew naturally out of that, really. She'd never been much of one for dating or having lots of boyfriends anyway.

As time went on she started wishing she'd done something a little more cultural and that she ought to do a night course or something like that, just to see if she'd like it. She had a look at the WEA website and didn't fancy some of the really difficult ones on books and philosophy, so she'd opted for art, as it was mostly looking at pictures anyway.

Steve hadn't liked it from the first. Instinctively she looked over at him, now slumped in his seat and snoring quietly. He was a good man – a really good man, she thought, compared with the couple of losers she'd been involved with before, and the sex, from what little previous experience she could judge, was really good. But he was just...well...he just didn't seem to have that many interests in common with her.

Karen cringed as she recalled trying, tentatively, to discuss the subject with her mum. She, just like the one or two friends she'd confided in, had said that Karen would be mad to turn down someone like Steve.

'Well I think he's a lovely man. And he's got a good job.' Mrs Kay had said, crossing her arms defensively in her frilly kitchen after plonking a mug of brick-red tea and a French Fancy in front of Karen.

'I can't think what you mean when you say you're not sure if you have anything in common. You get on alright, don't you?'

'Of course mum, but it's just...'

'Just what? You think I have anything in common with your dad?' Karen looked in the direction of the lounge where her father was sleeping in his armchair, the snooker balls silently rolling on the television screen in front of him.

Mrs Kay laughed and licked crumbs of cake from her fingers.

'He likes his snooker, and his fishing. I like reading romances and doing the garden. We get on alright. You girls these days, waiting for Mr Perfect to come along. Well believe me, he won't. You're 28 now and haven't had any kids. You don't want to end up like those career girls, putting it off until they're too old and having to have IMF treatment.'

'I*V*F treatment.' Karen looked sullenly into her tea mug.

'Whatever. Anyway, you play your cards right and you and Steve will get married or at least have kids. Just be thankful for what you got, that's what I say.'

Karen shook herself out of her reverie and tried to stretch a bit before she settled down to sleep. She snuggled up to Steve but he was sleeping deeply now, and shrugged off her embrace without waking.

****

Pauline handed her tray back to the plastic-gloved stewardess with a polite smile but Angie thrust her barely touched meal at her.

'That was terrible' said Angie. 'Can't you get me a boiled egg and toast instead?'

Pauline pretended to be interested in the TV screen in front of her while wishing the slippery plastic seat would swallow her up. She could still hear what was going on despite wearing headphones.

I'm sorry madam,' replied the stewardess. Her heavy makeup seemed to be the only thing holding her smile in place. 'But we can only serve the one meal unless you requested a vegetarian option.' The stewardess briskly swept the contents of the tray into the bin on her trolley, and turned to go.

Angie tutted. She grabbed the stewardess' arm and with a rattle of jewellery stabbed Pauline's LCD screen, causing a dark blob to spread momentarily across it.

'And this thing's not working proper either. It only shows the one film, and I've seen it already, and it were no good even then'.

'I'm sorry madam' said the stewardess through gritted teeth. 'You have to pay for our entertainment package if you want to see other films. It's priced at £14.99. We can take cards or cash.'

Angie tutted again. 'I'm not paying 15 pound to see Mr Bean prancing about. You could've at least asked us what film we wanted to see when we booked, so that we could express a preference.

The stewardess pretended not to hear and turned away to begin serving coffee.

'Never mind,' said Pauline brightly, taking off her headphones and hoping to silence Angie before she annoyed the stewardess even more. She'd heard of terrible things being done to the drinks if you got on the wrong side of these people. 'Why don't we have a bit of a nap instead? Then we'll be a bit fresher when we arrive. Or have one of your nicotine tablets. We've got eight hours to go, remember.'

'Eight more hours in this tin can,' wailed Angie. 'That's 12 hours altogether. I tell you I'm not flying long haul again. We'd have been better off in Spain.'

'Well when *you* booked the holiday, you said Spain was getting too common.'

'We should have booked Portugal instead. We'll be lucky we don't get that thing that you get with your legs on long haul flights.'

'What thing with your legs on long haul flights?' Pauline was worried now.

Angie tried to recall some medical term from a dimly remembered tabloid scare story.

'Deep Pan Thrombosis.'

Pauline shivered and tried to force herself to sleep as the sounds of drunken laughter and singing rose up from the back of the plane.

****

Ian sat indignantly in the stuffy heat of the lobby of the Las Cantatas hotel as he waited to check in. There was some sort of problem about his booking and they had to fetch someone. He fingered the purple plastic wristband the man on reception had insisted he had to put on, next to the beaded tribal wristlet he'd got in Cambodia. God only knew what it was for, it looked like the sort of thing people wore in hospital, but he noticed that all the guests seemed to have them. *Probably can't trust them not to lose everything,* he thought, considering the drunken state some of the guests seemed to be in at this relatively early hour.

He looked around disbelievingly at the tacky decor of the reception lobby. He couldn't believe the place was only about ten years old. It had the look of a cross channel ferry from the 1980s. The white concrete walls were scuffed and the doors black with kick marks. Cane armchairs with faded, overstuffed cushions in a jazzy design lined the walls and there was a strong smell of bleach rising from the floor.

A small minimarket at one end of the room was stuffed with sun tan lotion, cheap sunglasses and various novelty items featuring the union jack or topless women. A beach towel was for sale in the window, with the slogan 'My parents went on holiday and all they got me was a San Itairi towel'. Ian wondered if it was meant to be funny. A blackboard by the entrance proclaimed in large chalked letters 'Karaoke 2nite: pool bar!' On one wall a huge TV screen next to a bar showed a football match, the commentator's voice rising to a gabbling climax as a goal was scored.

A lone man dressed only in shiny white shorts and trainers leapt to his feet from one of the cane chairs and brandished a beer bottle at the screen, his beer belly wobbling with the movement.

'Yes, what a goal!' he shouted at the top of his voice, looking round for some sort of reaction from the rest of the bar. Finding it empty he slumped back down and sullenly continued drinking from his bottle.

Never mind, Ian told himself. *Just stay in your room, it's only one night. There's hardly anyone here anyway.*

At that moment the obese woman he'd seen at the airport came in from the terrace, with the little girl in tow. The woman was still in her black dress but the little girl had changed into a tiny red bikini, her thin body serving only to highlight the parody of adult clothing. The girl stopped at the minimarket and pressed her nose against the glass, looking longingly at a large plastic doll in what Ian assumed must be San Itairian national costume. The woman pulled her away.

'Come on Lianne. I told you we're going to the pool bar.'

The little girl looked crestfallen.

'But mum, can't I have one of them dolls?'

'You can have a slap, if you don't get a move on' barked her mother.

The woman noticed Ian looking at them. Before he could turn away, she scowled at him and led her daughter through the double doors out to the pool. Her shoulder tattoo wobbled in time with the ponderous slapping of her flip flops on the floor.

What is keeping them? Ian thought. He just wanted to get to his room. At that moment a middle aged, heavily made up woman with blonde hair and what looked like it might once have been a good figure arrived. She clacked across the floor in high heels and a turquoise coloured dress which looked like some sort of uniform. She had a conversation in pidgin English with the receptionist and then clacked over to Ian, gripping a clipboard firmly. The smell of her overpowering perfume hit him in the back of the throat.

'Well, well, well, hello stranger, thought you'd got left on the plane!' She eyed him up and down. 'Well you look very smart – at least you can't have got run over!'

'Erm...sorry?' He wondered if he was supposed to know this woman. She sounded like she knew *him*.

'I'm Trisha, I work for Solarflair. You're Ian? Ian Hurst?'

'Yes – is everything alright with my room?'

'Everything's fine my love – we was just wondering what had happened to you as we couldn't find you at the airport. We waited half an hour for you but you didn't turn up for the coach. Did you have a problem with customs? They haven't been strip searching again have they?'

She shrieked with laughter and touched his arm. 'I'm sorry, I can't help it. I get like this with good looking men. Don't I, Fuego?' She called across to the receptionist who nodded his head and smiled.

What is this woman on about? Ian thought, then suddenly realised he must be on some list because of the hotel booking that came with the flight.

'Ah, right, sorry,' faltered Ian, then thought *why am I apologising?* 'Yes there's been a bit of a mix up, I'm not supposed to be here.'

Trisha looked as if a favourite pet had just died, and seemed to try to speak more formally. 'Oh, I'm sorry, I've got your name down and registered for a week's all inclusive. We're just getting your room ready at this time. Don't worry, you haven't missed anything. I'm doing rep's welcome tomorrow and we've got karaoke in the...'

Ian cut her off abruptly. 'It's fine. I'm only here for one night – then I'm going back to London. Can you just make sure that's all in order. I'm booked on the one o' clock flight tomorrow.'

Trisha flipped over the pages on her clipboard. 'Yes, I see, yes it's all ok. You *are* booked on the flight tomorrow.' She sounded puzzled.

Ian sighed with relief. 'Good. Is my room ready now? I'd like to get some work done. I take it you have wi-fi?'

Trisha laughed and touched him on the arm again. 'I'm sorry, at this point in time we aren't able to provide that service. We do have an internet room but you'll have to book in with reception. I must say, I don't think we've ever had anyone ask for wi-fi. I'm quite impressed actually. May I ask what it is you do yourself?'

What on earth has it got to do with you? Ian was about to say, but checked himself. He really hadn't encountered anything like this before and realised he hadn't quite got over the voyeuristic shock of seeing the man dying on the road. The staff in the big hotels he stayed in for work kept a polite distance, but this woman seemed to treat him like a house guest. That was fine in small *pensiones* when he was on holiday; he expected that, but this woman was English and he thought she'd know it was intrusive.

'I'm a bit tired – I think I'd just like to go to my room now. I'm a bit...we saw a...never mind, I'd just like to lie down for a bit'.

'Oh-ho, a mystery man, eh? I like that. I think you must have been on a secret mission this morning, James Bond, you look done in! Come on, I'll show you to your room. I expect you'll want a wash and a shave.'

Ian stroked his carefully cultivated week-old beard with annoyance as Trisha babbled on.

'... then I've got to dash to the airport as it's changeover day and another lot are arriving. As I've already reiterated, I'll be doing my rep's welcome in the pool bar tomorrow so don't miss it'.

Ian had no idea what a 'rep's welcome' was and didn't want to know. 'That won't be necessary. Really.'

'All right then. Come on, I'll take you to your room, but I'm keeping my eye on you, secret agent 007!'

She shrieked with laughter again. 'Rep's welcome tomorrow Darren, I've got my eye on you and all,' she called to the topless man slumped in the corner. 'If this one's James Bond you must be Oddjob!'

Trisha cackled at her own joke and Darren grunted a reply without turning away from the game on the enormous TV screen.

She clacked off down the hallway as Ian followed behind, struggling to balance his case and laptop bag. The receptionist didn't seem interested in helping.

****

Trisha stood with a fixed smile in the arrivals terminal of the airport. She held up her clipboard with a photocopied Solarflair logo on it. It was coming to the end of the season and she hoped this would be the last one she had to do, stuck on this rock in the middle of nowhere having to be polite and fix the problems of the obnoxious tattoo-and-scar brigade that got flown in once or sometimes even twice a day from England.

When she'd signed up to be a rep she'd been expecting to spend her time in Spain or Portugal, with lots of sun and home only a couple of hours away, able to visit see her mum and friends but not her useless, now ex, boyfriend Warren. When Solarflair had opened the San Itairi resort she'd reluctantly agreed to go because the money was better and a couple of seasons would give her a chance to save up a bit before giving up repping and starting a business back home – preferably something not involving people.

That had been ten years ago. Somehow she'd got stuck in a rut. Perhaps not a rut exactly, but something between a rut and...what was it called? A 'comfort zone'. San Itairi was sunny and cheap, but a long way from home, and to counter the loneliness she'd had a string of what she politely called 'romances' with a succession of hotel staff, local men and, though it was risky, with hotel guests. She'd somehow never met the Tom Conti figure she'd been looking for. Now she was pushing 50 and the attention from men was starting to droop, as were the parts of her anatomy that attracted them.

Anyway, she might not have much choice about going home soon. The recession had hit long haul package holidays hard. In the boom years, when the banks had been willing to throw money at anybody with a pulse, British people had been having two or sometimes three holidays a year in places like San Itairi, plus weddings and even stag and hen dos, and Solarflair had the monopoly on accommodation and the beach because the President didn't want any new small places to be built. Not that anyone would have wanted to stay in them anyway, she thought. No pool or entertainment, why would they bother?

Now however the visitors had started to tail off, the hotel was in need of repair with much of it closed up, and to top it all, things were starting to get nasty on the island. Only this morning some politician had been killed on the main road and there were rumours that the whole place was about to go Egyptian.

She just hoped that she wouldn't be among Solarflair's planned 800 redundancies. *Actually,* she thought, *maybe that wouldn't be so bad.* A nice big payout and a flight back to Britain and no more stupid complaints. She might even get to mix with a better class of person. Like that bloke, what was his name, Ian, the one who missed the coach. Talked a bit posh, but good looking and those clothes cost a bit, she could tell.

She wondered vaguely what he was doing here; he didn't seem the usual type and he was on his own. James Bond! He looked a bit like him and all, though a bit thinner, and with stubble and specs. She'd have to check him out when he was round the pool. Suddenly she wondered if he was an inspector – she'd heard Solarflair did that sometimes, sent inspectors round to check on things undercover. That would make things *really* difficult if he was. She'd have to play this one really cool.

****

Karen and Steve finally located the holiday rep in the chaotic airport terminal. They had their names crossed off a list and they were directed to a coach on the far side of the shimmering car park. Karen noticed some groups of angry looking men milling around the taxi ranks, some of them in heated discussion with one another, being closely watched by policemen and soldiers, and wondered what could be going on.

A small, limping man in a short sleeved shirt swung their cases with practiced ease into the underside of the coach. Karen noticed suddenly that his left arm was missing below the elbow, and turned away quickly so that he wouldn't think she was staring. They boarded and found an empty pair of seats, nodding to some of the other tourists who had been sitting near them on the plane. Steve closed his eyes as he sank into the seat and they waited for the other passengers to board. The heat was oppressive.

'Thank God that flight's over. I just want to get to the hotel and get my head down for a bit' said Steve.

Karen got out her copy of the *Radical Planet Guide to the Caribbean* and started flicking to the pages on San Itairi. She murmured in agreement. 'Me too, I'm exhausted.' The guide book, the only one she'd been able to find in WH Smith's, didn't seem that complimentary about San Itairi. She was beginning to wonder if there would be enough to do there for a fortnight. Without thinking she exclaimed as she saw a section on the art gallery in San Itairi Town.

'Oh, it says here that Miguel Corantes lives on the island.'

Steve answered without opening his eyes. 'Who does he play for?'

'He's not a footballer. I've heard of him, he's an artist, it's in my book.'

'Not that again.'

Karen decided to keep talking about it, but realised she would have to tread carefully.

'It says there's two galleries in the town but they don't have any of his paintings. Oh well, might still be worth a look'.

Steve opened his eyes. 'Suit yourself, but I'm not going. I had enough of art in that place we went to in London.'

Karen laughed as she recalled their visit to the Tate Modern where Steve had almost knocked over one of the installations.

'Calling a load of dead flowers on the floor art – I nearly trod on them before I realised they were meant to be there. And that whooshing noise playing in the background, that wasn't art either.'

'Well...it's...conceptual art,' said Karen, falteringly. 'It's just as proper as anything else. That's what they say, anyway'.

'Well they would, wouldn't they? And people like you fall for it.'

Karen decided it was best to change the subject. 'I wonder what's keeping them, surely we're all here by now?'

She looked out of the window across the tarmac to see two overweight middle aged women struggling with their cases across the car park, following the blowsy-looking rep whose heels were clacking loudly across the tarmac. One of the women appeared to be complaining to the rep who was maintaining a fixed professional smile on her face and seemed to be ignoring her as best she could.

Eventually the two women boarded the coach and made their way to the only free seats at the rear of the coach. One of them, the argumentative one, was so fat that she had to sway her body from side to side as she moved along the narrow aisle, puffing angrily as the other woman followed meekly behind.

The small, one-armed man who had loaded the cases got into the driving seat and Karen realised he was the driver. She nudged Steve and pointed, and noticed that some of the other passengers were looking a bit concerned as well. A weasel-faced man in a baseball cap leant over the aisle and spoke in a loud Yorkshire accent to nobody in particular.

'What's he going to steer with when he wants to use his mobile?'

He then guffawed at his own joke. Karen gave a brief smile at the man and turned away. She didn't think it was funny to laugh at that kind of thing, but she did wonder how he was going to be able to drive the coach.

With a hiss the doors closed and the engine started, and a blast of musty smelling but blessedly cool air came out from the overhead ventilators. The coach pulled out of the car park and was soon bumping its way along a badly maintained dual carriageway which was perilously close to a cliff edge. The driver was clinging on to the wheel with grim determination.

The rep stood up at the front of aisle and blew into a microphone.

'Here we go' said Steve. 'Here comes the commercial. Wake me up when it's over.' He closed his eyes and leaned back in his seat.

Karen listened politely as the rep gave her welcome speech; she noticed that a few passengers around her were either asleep or ignoring her completely. It was like those safety announcements on the plane, she thought. You knew exactly what they were going to say but somehow it seemed rude not to at least pretend you were interested.

'Right then ladies and gentlemen, hello everyone!'

The rep looked around expectantly and a few passengers murmured a greeting.

'That's not very good is it? I said, hello!' The woman cupped her hand around her ear and leaned forward. This time the response was a bit louder. Satisfied, she continued with her speech.

'Welcome to the lovely island of San Itairi! My name is Trisha, and I'm your Solarflair representative. Our driver is Stephano. Now some of you may have noticed Stephano has only one arm, but don't worry – he's been driving buses along the cliff road for many a year and no-one's died yet…although there was the one heart attack last year but I'm assured the gentlemen is doing as well as can be expected. What you might not have noticed is Stephano only has one leg! Isn't it wonderful what they can do with prosthetics these days - but don't worry – the coach has automatic transmission.

'Now, you're all going to be staying at the lovely all inclusive resort of Las Cantatas. There's a lovely private beach, a great pool and wonderful entertainment every night– there's almost no need to leave the resort, but don't forget we do a lot of great trips around the island which I'll be telling you about later.

'A couple of points first though. Now, you may have heard all sorts of rumours in the papers about the political situation here in San Itairi. Yes, some flights back to the UK have been cancelled due to industrial action and there is a taxi strike but I can assure you, ladies and gentlemen, that we're not about to have a revolution here on the island! So just sit back, enjoy the scenery, and we'll be at the resort in just under an hour.'

There was a collective groan from the passengers and Karen could hear the fat woman who'd got on last start to complain to her companion, but she couldn't make out the exact words.

The coach lurched to the left to overtake a lorry and the woman turned to face the front of the coach. She shouted a warning as a small white car almost hit them, swerving out of the path of the coach at the last minute.

'Stephano, watch out for that hire car! Bloody tourists!'

****

Pauline woke up as the coach turned off the main road onto a bumpy unmade road. She saw a sign for 'Las Cantatas Resort' and realised they were nearly there. *This looks nice*, she thought, as the late afternoon sun slanted over the low white buildings dotted with palm trees, with the hazy blue sea stretching out beyond. Tired as she was, she was really starting to look forward to the holiday.

Angie had nodded off as well, but suddenly came to as the coach hit a pothole. Pauline nudged her and said brightly, 'we're nearly here, Ange. It looks nice.'

'I'll believe that when I see it. How can it take this long to go across a tiny island? We must have travelled 60 miles to go five.'

Pauline wasn't quite sure if that made sense. 'I think they had to go slow because of the roads. They're a bit bumpy'.

'It's not the roads, it's that one armed bandit in charge of this charabanc that's the problem. That's the first thing I'm mentioning when I write my review.' Angie pointed at the driver.

'Ssh, he'll hear you. He can't help that, he's doing his best'.

Angie carried on moaning. Pauline tried to distract her. 'I had a look at that duty free shop in the airport as well, while you were in the toilet.'

Pauline brightened. 'Oh yes, remind me I want to bring back 400 fags when we go home'.

'You can't, they only let you take 200 here. The girl said it was a rule from the British customs. Our government seems to treat us like kids, don't they?'

Angie frowned. 'Well don't blame me, you know I don't vote. And another thing, that rep girl didn't help with our cases either. Swanning around the airport like Judith Chalmers. I'm not going to her welcome talk either, I tell you that.'

'Why not? It might be quite interesting. They tell you what to see and all sorts in those meetings.'

'No they don't, they just try to sell you trips. What's the point of going on a trip when you're on holiday? You're already on a trip.'

The coach stopped outside the hotel's main entrance and the passengers began alighting. Angie began elbowing her way forward to the doors as Pauline smiled apologetically at a young couple who gave way to them.

The first of the straggling group of tourists began wheeling their cases across the waste ground to the Las Cantatas Hotel.

****

From the main coast road that the coach had travelled along, a long, dusty column of army lorries and armoured vehicles, filled with sullen conscripts, lurched and swayed its way towards San Itairi Town.

Four

Ian sat on the small terrace which was shared by two neighbouring hotel rooms on either side. At first he had tried to stay in his room to start work on his article, but the intense heat (there was no air conditioning) had driven him outside to the relative coolness of the terrace. He would have liked to have gone to some secluded spot on the beach but his battery was running low, so he stayed close to the dangerous looking blackened plug socket by his room door and fiddled with the 3g settings on his laptop to try to get some sort of internet access.

Nothing seemed to work and his phone had packed up as well, so he resigned himself to getting some work done on his article before dinner and then bed. He was just thankful that nobody seemed to be occupying the neighbouring rooms, giving him some privacy and sparing him from having to witness any more of the horrors of the hotel.

He hadn't explored the place and didn't want to – he'd seen enough on his walk from reception to his room while passing the pool area. It was hard to believe places like this *actually* existed. Growing up, he'd spent his holidays in Tuscany or Umbria or Provence at the homes of various academic colleagues of his parents, where over wine and good food the debates over art, literature and politics would go on long into the night.

He and Jenny most summers would go on city breaks to new and exciting places, usually with a gritty, edgy and urban feel, where, despite being in a hotel, you could still experience what life was really like for local people.

There was some sort of karaoke contest going on there on the stage. The person in charge was a tarty woman in a union jack dress who looked like a superannuated Spice Girl. She was belting out Whitney Houston's *I Will Always Love You* with a variety of blood curdling vocal gymnastics that made him wince. Ian could still hear her from his terrace and it seemed the entire competition consisted of just her singing that song or an equally bad version of Robbie Williams' *Angels*.

He'd also caught a glimpse of the 'restaurant' which looked more like a staff canteen in a very down at heel factory. People in various states of undress were milling around with trays looking at a selection of unappetising fried food under orange lights, or slouched eating chips at tables littered with half-eaten food and dirty plates, while the staff made half hearted attempts to wipe down the surfaces.

Everywhere there was noise and heat, and groups of rowdy children racing around unsupervised. He'd never seen so many baby buggies and young children in one place before and at the back of his mind he wondered whether it was true that some of these people had children just to get benefit money, but squashed the thought with horror. *You write for the* Daily Defender, *not the* Daily Mail, he told himself. *Just ignore them and get on with your work.*

He started to feel better as he realised it was only for one night anyway, by tomorrow morning he would be out and back to London and normality. He would put off his article on Corantes until he was on the plane, but do a short piece for the paper on the assassination of the opposition politician. Once he got 3g coverage he could either phone or email the report through to London, although he guessed somebody else had probably done it by now, he would be able to give plenty of detail and had even got a picture of the body. He had a flash of inspiration and decided to contrast the island's political situation with the oblivious atmosphere of the Las Cantatas Hotel.

He began typing. *Behind the facade of a happy holiday resort, could the authoritarian government of the tiny Caribbean island of San Itairi be heading for its long deserved downfall?* He paused. Was 'long deserved' too biased? Perhaps he should put 'long awaited'.

Then he considered a different approach. His fingers flew over the keys like Rick Wakeman playing the piano. *Bingo and karaoke are the order of the day for British holidaymakers in happy camper land at the tacky Las Cantatas Resort in San Itairi, while the island's workers struggle against an authoritarian government thought to be complicit in the assassination of...*he paused. That might come across as snobbish, and that wouldn't do. People might also wonder why he was mixing with these sorts of people instead of staying with Corantes, and that *definitely* wouldn't do.

However, he realised he had to get some sense of decadent westerners enjoying themselves at the expense of exploited local labour. Typing quickly he began to sweat and cursed the heat, wishing that the shoddy hotel had been built properly with air conditioning.

Before he could type much more he heard the rumbling of suitcase wheels and looked up to see a young couple walking along the terrace towards him. The man nodded at him and the woman smiled and said hello, then they both went into the room to the left of Ian's and closed the door. He could hear the sounds of subdued conversation and cases being opened. He'd hoped he'd have the terrace to himself but perhaps not; anyway they didn't look too bad; the man obviously a bit thick but the girl seemed friendly enough and not bad looking either. Definitely an improvement on the horrors he'd seen lounging around the pool, anyway. Ian's journalistic experience had taught him the ability to sum up people pretty well at first glance and they didn't seem the noisy type. He settled back into the rhythm of typing.

If you remember the 1980s TV series Hi De Hi *then you'll know just what it's like in the Las Cantatas resort on San Itairi. If you're unlucky enough to be one of the island's underpaid workers,* Tenko *might be a more appropriate comparison.*

He stopped typing and deleted the paragraph. This wasn't something to be flippant about and besides, he suspected that ironic references to TV programmes that nobody under 40 would remember might make him sound like some minor celebrity on a Channel Five nostalgia programme. *You'll be writing about Spangles and space hoppers next. Keep it focused on the issues*, he thought.

He tried the 3g again but still it didn't work. If this carried on, he realised grimly that he would have to visit the internet room. Before he could begin typing again he was interrupted by the sound of suitcase wheels, as a couple of women in late middle age rounded the corner and crossed the terrace to the free room on the right of his.

The woman in front was gaudily dressed in baggy shorts and some sort of flowery nylon blouse. She had the face of an angry bulldog topped with a badly bleached, spiky hairdo which was wilting in the heat. She ignored him as she briskly opened the door of the room and bustled inside. A smaller, apologetic woman followed and gave Ian a quick smile as she hurried past. The door closed and he could hear a muffled, complaining voice, presumably from bulldog-face. Hoping that was the last of the distractions for this evening, Ian continued typing as the sounds of karaoke from the poolside gradually grew louder.

****

Karen was already feeling sticky only minutes after her shower and turned up the speed on the rickety ceiling fan in the hope that it might cool the room a little. Steve was still in the shower, singing along badly with the sounds of the karaoke drifting through the open bathroom window.

She always loved the start of a holiday, arriving in the hotel room and finally getting to see where she would be spending the next fortnight. She and Steve had been on a good number of decent package holidays and had got to see a lot of interesting places.

Growing up, holidays hadn't been much fun. The Kays had gone to the same place every year, a windswept desolate caravan park near Cleethorpes. Every year without fail, the family's decrepit Austin Maestro would break down from the strain of pulling the caravan and Karen and her mother would sit inside the car waiting for the engine to cool down as Mr Kay tinkered under the open bonnet. Karen would squirm with embarrassment as new, fast cars rushed past with girls her own age staring, and sometimes laughing, at their tatty convoy.

The autumn term at school was always embarrassing too, as her friends swapped blurry photos and stories of the amazing hotels they'd stayed in on holiday in places like Spain or Greece, boasting about huge blue pools, water slides, late night discos and snoggable lads. Karen later realised that their holidays were probably just cheap package deals but at the time, it seemed like an unreachable world of wealth and glamour.

Once she had tentatively asked mum and dad if they could stay in a hotel next year instead of the caravan, and had even got some brochures from a travel agent to show them. *The very idea,* her mother had scoffed. Hotels to Karen's mother meant those big wedding cake buildings on esplanades, that cost a fortune and where you had to mind your p's and q's and worry about what fork to use when you ate your tea. *No thank you, the caravan's good enough for us,* she had said, and that was final.

So ever since she was 18, Karen had gone abroad every year to somewhere sunny and interesting, in an attempt to recapture some of what she thought she'd missed in her teenage years. 'Gallivanting about' her mum called it, but Karen suspected she was secretly a bit jealous.

Not such a bad place, she thought, looking around at the room; *the place has seen better days but you can't expect much at this price*. The people she'd seen on the way in looked like a decent enough crowd, if a bit rough, but they all seemed to be enjoying themselves. She didn't mind karaoke and bingo now and then on holiday but she hoped that Steve would come round to the idea of a few walks around San Itairi town and perhaps some trips further afield. She didn't want to be out every day, after all she was on holiday, but it would be nice to see a bit of the island rather than just the hotel. She began to thumb through her guidebook to see what might be worth a look.

Realising she was only in her bra and knickers, she walked over to close the dusty venetian blinds over the window and saw the man outside looking at his laptop. He momentarily looked up as she clicked the blind shut. She wondered what he was doing – he looked like he should be in a trendy office somewhere. At least he didn't look like he'd be noisy – the walls looked pretty thin between these rooms.

She suddenly smiled to herself as she remembered that Steve had once joked that she was a 'screamer'. She was horribly embarrassed about that and really didn't think she made all that much noise in bed. Then her smile faded as she remembered it had been over a week since they'd made love. One or the other had been too tired or working a late shift. Sex was supposed to get better on holiday, she'd read somewhere, and she hoped that would be enough to lighten the recent difficult atmosphere between them. She'd asked Steve if he'd wanted to share a shower but he'd declined, saying the cubicle was too small.

She heard a buzzing then the sound of Steve's phone ringing by the bed. She was about to call out to him decided it would be quicker to take the phone over to the bathroom. Realising it might take a while for Steve to pick up she decide to answer before she passed the phone over.

'Hello?' There was no reply.

'Hello, Steve Trout's phone?'

The line went dead. Probably just some connection problem, she thought, but wondered who could be calling. She looked at the caller ID screen which said 'Anna.' *A bit odd*, she thought – she couldn't recall anyone called that. She felt a twinge of suspicion.

Steve emerged from the shower with a towel tied tightly round his middle.

'Your phone just rang,' said Karen. Without thinking she added a lie. 'I didn't have time to pick up though before they rang off'.

Steve looked surprised. 'Oh yeah? Who's that then? I'm not expecting anyone.'

He picked up his phone, glanced at it briefly then tucked it away in his clothing on the bed.

'Anything important?' Karen asked lightly.

Steve looked a bit flustered. 'Er, just a work thing. Doesn't matter.'

Karen was about to say that since they worked together Karen knew there was nobody called Anna at work; and anyway, why would work be calling him when they knew he was on holiday? She decided she didn't want to appear paranoid. She was really a bit suspicious now though. Perhaps it was someone work related that she didn't know, one of the printing clients who sometimes called the goods-in staff direct – that would explain why she didn't realise he was on holiday. But why had the woman hung up? Was it just a bad connection? *Or is he having some kind of...?* Unsettling thoughts started to appear in her mind and she suddenly desired Steve strongly.

'You don't need that towel Mr Prude. There's only the two of us here. Why don't you take it off?'

'You never know with these places who can see in. That bloke still typing out there?'

Karen lifted a corner of the blind to look at the terrace.

'I think he's gone in now, and anyway why would he want to look at you?'

'I meant he might want to look at you, not me.'

'Not if he's gay.' Karen laughed.

'Looks like he might be actually. Well he can look all he wants then, he won't be getting anything from me'. He whipped the towel off and bent over the bed to put on clean underwear.

'Hurry up and get dressed then,' urged Karen, pulling on her tee shirt and shorts. 'I'm starving, let's go and get something to eat'.

Steve hesitated. 'Er...can I catch you up? I've just remembered there's a match on, I want to catch the last few minutes'.

Karen was puzzled. He hadn't mentioned any match before. She'd hoped they could spend at least one evening together without football interrupting.

'Alright then, I'll have a starter in the restaurant and wait for you. Who's playing anyway?'

'Er...Barcelona I think. Yeah, Barcelona. Good team, worth a look.'

Karen could never understand what differentiated one team from another. It all looked the same to her. Steve had never been much interested in foreign teams before. The niggling suspicion in the back of her mind started up again and she felt an urgent need to be desired by Steve. She stroked the back of his hair.

'Well alright then, but don't take too long and no downing pints before dinner. I'd like you to still be in reasonable shape by bedtime.'

Steve held his hands up in mock protest.

'Alright, alright, I'll only have one pint. Think I'll get my head down early tonight though, get a good night's sleep.'

It looks like that's all I'll be getting as well then, thought Karen, as she finished her makeup.

'I was having a look at the guide book and it says the old town is quite interesting' said Karen, trying to sound nonchalant. 'There are one or two really old churches.'

Steve pulled on his t-shirt. 'Churches? What do you want to look at them for? Seen one, you've seen them all. You're not religious anyway.'

'You know I'm not religious, but the book says that there are one or two good paintings in the churches here. Church art is one of the modules on my course.'

'Church art? Christ. They're all just pictures of baby Jesus, aren't they? No thanks. I had enough of all that in church parade in the army. It's all made up, anyway.'

'What's all made up?'

'Churches, religion and that. All made up to...to keep people down'.

'How do you know that?'

'Read it, didn't I?'

Steve must have noted Karen's look of surprise as he continued. 'Yes, I read books sometimes as well you know. It was in that *Da Vinci Code* book.'

Karen remembered Steve had skimmed through a dog-eared copy of the bestseller he'd found in the hotel library on holiday last year. It was true he did read sometimes, but he only had a small collection of books about football and military stuff.

'Well I don't know if it's made up or not, how does anyone know? I just think it would be nice to see some paintings and a bit of culture, see something with a bit of historic atmosphere, that's all.'

Steve frowned. 'Look. I know you're doing this course and it's all about art and philosophy and what not, but as far as I see it, the only things that really matter in life are a good game of football, a good piss up, and a good...'

Steve's voice trailed away as he began to run his hands through Karen's hair. Suddenly she had a vision of the words 'Anna' on his phone and pushed him away.

Karen's voice trembled on the edge of tears as she hurried to the door. 'I'm going to the restaurant. You can come and meet me after your precious football if you think you can stand my company without having to take the piss out of me.'

She slammed the door on Steve as he looked at her in puzzlement and surprise.

****

As dusk fell over the island and the crickets began their nightly chorus, Miguel carefully locked the door of his studio and drew the blinds. He had seen on the TV news about the assassination of the opposition politician, who he had known quite well. The news had claimed he was killed while resisting arrest and had tried to shoot a police officer, but of course that was all state propaganda. Miguel realised now had to be the time to act, before it was too late and they came for him as well. He went into a darkened corner and carefully unwrapped what he had shown Ian, a plan forming in his mind.

Outside in the dark, a car containing four armed men turned off the main road and descended slowly along the country lane to the studio. The driver switched off his headlights and let in the clutch to cruise silently down the hill to the lonely building.

Five

Angie burst out of the room onto the terrace, followed by Pauline who was trying unsuccessfully to placate her. Angie had obviously been unhappy with the room since she first saw it, and Pauline's attempts at avoiding a fuss had finally come to nothing.

'I don't care Pauline, I'm not stopping in that room a moment longer, I'm stopping out here where I can breathe.'

She lit a cigarette and pointed in the direction of the hotel reception. 'Go and get that rep.'

Pauline tried to smile. 'Look, aren't you going over the top a bit Angie? It's only a bit of mould in the bathroom. Only needs a bit of bleach.'

Angie exhaled a cloud of smoke angrily. 'A bit of mould? A bit of bleach? That shower curtain practically had mushrooms on it! I told you they don't clean proper in these places. And foreign bleach isn't like ours so it wouldn't work the same. There's nothing for it, they're moving us or we're getting in compensation. And as for that business with the toilet paper – well, they can forget about that!'

She shivered with disgust and folded her arms, puffing and looking into middle distance the way outdoor smokers always seem to.

Pauline tried to explain. 'They said at reception – the plumbing can't cope with paper, so you have to put it in the bin. That's what it's there for. It was the same when Ron and I were in Greece. The sewers can't cope.'

Angie was not having any of it.

'I'm not putting used toilet paper in a bin! That might be alright for the locals, but they should have proper sewers for the tourists. What do they think this is – the third world?'

'Well if it gets blocked...'

'Then they can *un*block it. And just look at this.' Angie pointed to a shabby sun lounger on the terrace. Two of its legs were badly mended with dirty white electrical tape.

'What about it?' Pauline wondered if there was going to be anything that Angie *wouldn't* complain about.

Angie kicked one of the damaged legs and the chair scraped along the terrace with a loud scraping noise. 'Just look at the state of it! That leg's busted. Someone could have an accident on this. Look. I bet it won't take me weight.'

She plonked herself onto the lounger and began bobbing up and down as if testing a mattress. The chair momentarily supported her but then with a loud crack the lounger collapsed and Angie was thrown back with her legs in the air, helplessly trying to right herself like an upturned beetle. With a gasp of surprise she shouted at Pauline.

'Well don't just stand there, get a picture, get a picture of these legs!'

Pauline grabbed her camera and took a picture of Angie's lower half, the flash in the subdued evening light making her spread legs look even whiter than usual. Angie shouted angrily and managed to stand up, brushing imaginary dust off her shorts.

'Not of my legs, I mean of this broken leg on the lounger. That's evidence, that is'.

Pauline carefully took another picture of the chair leg while Angie touched her hairdo to ensure all was in place. She straightened up. 'Now, that's another thing on the list for that rep. Are you going to get her or do I have to?'

'Couldn't it wait until we've had our tea? I'm dead hungry and you must be as well,' answered Pauline, hopefully.

Angie slammed her fist on the white plastic table, making the ashtray jump and spill black dust everywhere.

'No Pauline – get her now. We had this out last year. When your Ron died I agreed to come on holiday with you. I didn't go for me own sake, I went because I thought you'd like the company after your husband died because I knew how it felt as well. And how do I get repaid? You put up with substandard accommodation, same as last year. Well you can sort it out!'

Pauline cringed and decided it would be best to sort it out after all. Angie sounded like she certainly wasn't just going to forget about it. She took a deep breath and began walking briskly towards the front desk.

Angie called out after her. 'I do sometimes wonder about your standards of hygiene you know. In fact I wonder if going on holiday with friends is such a good idea at all!'

'So do I, Angie, so do I,' whispered Pauline to herself, through gritted teeth.

****

The temperature in Ian's room was now almost bearable and he had finished his article on the assassination, despite the noise of that woman next door. She'd been complaining about something but he couldn't make out what, so decided to block her and the ever present dirge from the karaoke out with some Coldplay on his iphone. He had given up on trying to get his laptop or phone to get a signal, and decided that the best course of action would be to take his data stick to the internet room and send it from there. With a bit of luck and the time difference it would make tomorrow's issue of the *Defender* or at least get put on the website.

He felt his stomach give an unpleasant lurch and realised he hadn't eaten for hours. *God only knows what the food in this place would be like,* he thought – his glimpse of the restaurant had been less than appetising. He thought at first of going into town, finding a little taverna somewhere with some seafood and white wine; something local and authentic, but then dismissed the thought; it was a long taxi ride and he had an early start for the plane tomorrow. He decided he would make a last attempt at getting a 3g signal outside then if that failed he would check out the internet room. After that he would risk the restaurant.

Blessedly cool air greeted him as he opened the door onto the terrace so he shrugged on his jacket and set up his laptop on the grubby white table on the terrace. With a surge of joy he noticed that his 3g status showed as 'connecting', and a small green bar was slowly creeping across the indicator dial as the computer struggled to connect with the weak signal. He noticed a woman standing on the terrace outside the room next door, smoking and looking at him. It was 'Bulldog face', the complaining woman. *What a sight*. He'd once heard a description of a woman who had a face 'like a bulldog licking piss off a nettle'. Sexist of course, but very true in this case. He ignored her as he made the final touches to his article before he sent it off.

''Scuse me love,' called the woman, forebodingly.

Could he just ignore her, he wondered? If he'd had his headphones on then he could have just pretended he hadn't heard her...then again, he thought it might be best not to antagonise people like that.

'Yes?' He answered coldly, aware that her gaze was boring into him and that she had blocked his path off the terrace.

'Are you working here?'

What has it got to do with her? Ian thought, but then felt the need to assert himself as being separate to all this; as bizarre as it sounded he didn't want this woman thinking he was actually on holiday in this dump.

'Actually yes, I am working. I've got to send some urgent emails now, so if you don't mind...'

The woman folded her arms. 'Right then, if you work here, I want a word with you. We've got a problem with our room.'

Ian had to stop himself from bursting out laughing. Did she seriously think he worked here? Like some sort of Butlins manager? He decided this woman needed to be firmly put in her place.

'You don't understand. I am working here, but I don't work for this hotel. I'm a journalist, I'm writing an article and I need to send it to my paper in

London, so if you'll excuse me...'

Before he could look back at the laptop screen he was surprised to see the woman's face crack into a ghastly smile, revealing nicotine-stained teeth.

'Oh, write for a paper, do you? Which one?'

Ian noticed the green indicator bar had barely moved. Best to give it a few more minutes, he thought.

'*The Daily Defender*'.

The woman's face looked blank. 'I suppose that's one of the big ones. I don't read them myself. Nice to meet someone who works for one though. I've always fancied myself as a bit of a writer.'

Oh Christ, groaned Ian inwardly. He got this occasionally when people found out he was a journalist. It usually ended up with them asking if he would take a look at their 'humble scribblings' in the hope that he'd actually print their amateurish ramblings.

The woman moved to the table and sat down opposite next to Ian, without being invited, and ineffectually waved her cigarette smoke away from his direction. Ian noticed her voice seemed to have adopted a more genteel tone.

'Yes, as I say, I do a bit of writing meself from time to time'. She pronounced it almost as 'tame to tame', and Ian noticed she was craning her neck to look at his screen. He felt his anger rise as the green indicator barely moved. Was the bloody thing ever going to connect?

There was a pause, and Ian realised she was probably waiting for him to ask what sort of writing she did. *Well she can wait*, he thought. Finally the green bar filled the dial and a box appeared on the screen to announce the computer was now connected to the 3g network. Ian hurriedly typed out a covering email and attached his article, then sent the message to his newsroom, sitting back in the wobbly plastic chair with a sigh of relief. His attitude to the woman softened a little.

'Really, you're a writer? How fascinating.' He gave a sly smile which seemed to encourage the woman. She obviously didn't notice his very subtle ironic tone.

'Well, I wouldn't say I were a *writer* exactly. I do the odd little review now and then. For websites about hotels, that sort of thing. When something needs putting right, you know.'

Ian suddenly remembered the muffled sounds of complaint he'd heard from the woman's room. *Professional complainer, obviously*, he thought. *Probably writes those semi-literate rants on websites like Travel Advisor.*

The woman stubbed her cigarette out and carried on talking.

'I'll be sending a little review to Travel Advisor when this holiday's over. And it won't be complimentary I can tell you. This place is a dump.'

Ian chuckled as he began to shut down his computer. 'I'd agree with you there.'

A look of satisfaction crossed the woman's face. She looked as if she'd found a kindred spirit.

'I'm glad someone does. My friend thinks it's OK and nobody else seems bothered either. I can tell you've got higher standards though. Are you from London? You look like you might be'.

'Yes, I am, as a matter of fact'.

She looked puzzled. 'But you don't have a cockney accent. You sound quite classy.'

Ian was a bit put out. Since his schooldays Ian had honed his accent to perfection; classless, with just the right sound on the glottal stops, like Tony Blair. A London accent which he could strengthen when it was required, but he'd hoped it never sounded 'classy'.

'We don't all have cockney accents in London.'

The woman nodded and Ian wondered if she'd understood. He soon realised she hadn't.

'Oh right. I suppose what with all those foreigners there, you get all sorts of accents.'

Ian sighed. The woman carried on talking.

'Thought you must be from London though when I saw that posh jacket. Where's it from, Marks?'

Ian felt a mixture of hilarity and pity welling up inside him. 'Oswald Boateng, actually'. He'd got it as a freebie when he'd done a feature on racism in men's tailoring.

'Fits nicely. Could have been made for you'.

'It was.'

The woman raised an eyebrow and lit another cigarette. Just as he was about to close his email account, Ian noticed a message and his heart sank as he read 'internal server error: unable to deliver your message'. He tried to resend but then saw the 3g connection was broken and repeated clicks failed to elicit any response. He snapped the lid of the laptop shut in disgust.

'If you'll excuse me I'd better go. I'm going to have to use the internet room.'

'Righto love. If you see me friend tell her to hurry up with that rep, and if you want any extra info for your article you come to me.' She tapped the side of her nose.

Ian hurriedly secreted his laptop in his room and locked the door, ignoring the woman's request, mainly as he hadn't a clue what she was rambling on about. He pocketed his usb stick and strode in the direction of the internet room.

****

Trisha clacked briskly through the pool bar, past the queue of people waiting to get to the restaurant. *I could do without this*, she thought. With the situation at the airport worsening she was having to cope with angry crowds wanting their rooms in the hotel back. She couldn't understand why they couldn't just kip down on the floor at the airport anyway. And now this woman was saying she, or rather her friend, had a problem with their room.

Pauline explained apologetically again. 'It's only a bit dirty, love, that's all, nothing really, but my friend, well she has allergies you see...'

Trisha kept up her brisk pace and fixed smile. 'Dealing with problems is not a problem at all, that's what I'm here for'. If that bloke in the room next to them really was a hotel inspector she was going to have to be as professional as possible.

As they approached the terrace Trisha noticed the bulldog-faced woman who she'd heard complaining on the coach. *Oh God*. She looked like one of the sort who thinks a three star package resort should have the same standards as the Ritz.

'Here we are Angie, this girl's come about the room. This is my friend Angie.' Pauline smiled at Trisha and they nodded at each other. Trisha decided to soften Angie with a pre-emptive charm strike. She beamed a smile and consulted her clipboard.

'Hello there!' she said brightly. 'Your friend here says there's a little problem with some mould in the bathroom. Not a problem at all.'

Angie was not to be placated so easily.

'You took your time. And you haven't seen what I'm going to show you yet so don't start saying it's not a problem. I'll be the judge of that. Come through here'.

She led the way into the bathroom and the three of them squeezed in. Angie brandished the shower curtain and thrust it under Angie's nose.

'Just look at that. Mould all over it. You could grow mushrooms on that'.

Trisha maintained her calm professional manner as she wrinkled her nose and looked at the few spots of discolouration on the plastic curtain.

'I can assure you madam that a small amount of discolouration is normal on the fixtures and fittings, it's caused by the high humidity'.

Angie looked daggers at Trisha. 'Caused by the dirt, more like. I know the cleaners here are foreign and probably don't know owt better, but people like you should be setting an example.'

Trisha smiled. 'Shall we step out into the lounge area?'

The three women exited the bathroom. Trisha made a mark on her clipboard. 'There now, I've made a note to ask the cleaner to make an extra special effort tomorrow with some bleach. Will that be all, ladies?'

Angie lit a cigarette and pointed it accusingly at Trisha. 'You're not getting off that easily. The amount of bleach you'd need to clean that thing would cause an environmental disaster in here. Look at me, I'm gasping for breath as it is already!' She coughed as she took a drag on her cigarette.

Pauline stepped in and smiled at Trisha. 'Thanks love, I'm sure a bit of bleach will shift it.'

Angie ignored her. 'And another thing, the sun lounger on that terrace collapsed when I sat on it'.

Trisha looked away and said under her breath, 'I'm not surprised.'

Angie flushed a deep red. 'What was that?'

Trisha smiled reassuringly. She found that lots of jargon helped in these situations. 'I'm not surprised, it's clearly broken and not fit for purpose, and constitutes a contradiction of health and safety breaches, I shall make a note to have that replaced as soon as possible.' She scribbled minutely on her clipboard.' 'Now, is there anything else...'

Angie interrupted. 'Oh yes. Apparently it's too much to be able to flush paper down the toilet, but on the subject of which, there's only half a roll of paper here. Half a roll! If one of us gets the runs, that constitutes a medical emergency, and I'll be claiming compensation for, for...duty of care.'

Trisha's smile was under dangerous strain. She chirped brightly.

'Right then, I've made a note on the bleach, the chair, and the toilet tissue. I think that's all in order, so if you'll just bear with me, I'll be progressing on my way and can let you get on with enjoying your holiday going forward.' She stepped towards the door.

Angie barred her exit. 'You don't seem to understand love. Look, we want an upgrade. This room isn't...isn't fit for purpose. I've taken pictures of this and I'm sending them to your head office and putting them online. And it's not just me. There's a bloke next door doing a report on this place and all, so don't go thinking it's me being some silly old woman.'

For the first time Trisha's smile dropped. So he *was* an inspector then. Just her luck he'd come at the absolute worst time. She would have to make sure he was properly looked after instead of her wasting time on these two jokers.

'I'm very sorry madam,' she trilled, 'but at this time, there are no other rooms available at present, due to full bookings on the remainder of rooms that are left.'

Angie looked unconvinced. 'What do you mean, full bookings? This is the end of the season. Don't tell me every room is booked out here.'

A gleam of triumph crossed Trisha's face.

'Unfortunately I am sorry to regret to inform you that the hotel *is* fully booked. This is due to the industrial action at the airport which is causing a backlog of guests able to leave for their departure. But rest assured I will get all this sorted for you, in due course and as soon as possible'.

Pauline touched Trisha on the arm. 'Thanks love, we know you must be run off your feet.' Angie just grunted.

A bit of an odd couple, thought Trisha. In her experience you got guests who were either perfectly nice, or complete moaners, like bulldog-face, but you didn't often get them visiting together. She wondered why Pauline put up with it.

'Come on Pauline. Let's get to the buffet before they stop serving.' With a final flourish she looked at Trisha and said 'I just hope that's a bit cleaner than this place.'

They left the room and locked the door as Trisha made some final notes on her clipboard. 'Rest assured madam I will pass your comments on to the appropriate quarters.'

As Angie and Pauline left the terrace and turned the corner out of sight, Trisha tore the form off her clipboard, scrunched it into a ball and tossed it over the perimeter wall.

****

On the coast road, another column of trucks full of soldiers moved slowly towards the seashore at the far end of the beach, about half a mile away from the hotel. The soldiers jumped down from the lorries and hurriedly began erecting barbed wire fencing across the sands, moving swiftly and silently in the moonlight.

Six

Karen sat glumly in the restaurant. She had finished her starter and her first glass of wine, served to her by a bored looking waiter straight from a paper carton like the kind used for orange juice. Steve still hadn't arrived and she was starting to get annoyed. She looked at his empty place on the table in front of her. An elderly couple on the next table looked at her with concern and the woman leant over.

'Are you on your own love?'

Karen looked up with surprise. 'No, no, it's ok, my boyfriend's coming in a bit. He's just got held up I think.'

The woman seemed reassured. 'Oh well that's alright then love. You just looked a bit lonely.'

The man nodded his agreement and raised a huge glass of lager at her. 'Cheer up love, you're on holiday!'

Karen smiled weakly and looked away from them. The room was full to bursting with crowds of holidaymakers, mostly British but with a few Germans and, she guessed, Dutch in one corner, eating heartily with their faces growing ever more shiny and red. She decided she would get another helping of salad then go and look for Steve. There wasn't much of a queue at the salad bar, in a corner of the restaurant overlooking the steep path down to the beach.

She found herself gazing out into the darkness, noticing what seemed to be a column of vehicles parked at far end of the beach. She strained her eyes but could only see some dark figures moving about indistinctly in the distance. Then she recoiled in shock as she noticed two figures standing at the foot of the steps leading to the beach, dimly lit by small lamps set in the concrete.

It was Steve, and he was with a woman. She could just make out that she was very pretty, with dark hair and skin much darker than Steve's. Could she be a local girl? They seemed to be deep in conversation. She saw Steve laughing and pointing towards the beach, then he looked at his watch and pointed back to the hotel. She stepped quickly back into the restaurant in case he saw her, a quiver of anger welling up in her throat and tears pricking at her eyes.

She hurriedly walked back to her table and sat down, noting with relief that the well-meaning couple next to her had gone, to be replaced by a family guzzling chips and not paying her the slightest attention. *So that's his football*, she thought to herself as she ordered another glass of wine from the waiter.

She tried to think rationally but a mist of jealously kept clouding everything and a horrible, nagging voice in her mind kept whispering to her. The jetlag and wine and her empty stomach weren't helping either. *Surely he couldn't be*...they'd only just arrived so how did he have time to meet some woman...? Then she remembered the call on his mobile from 'Anna'. He must have known her already, she realised. Had he set this whole holiday up to meet some woman? But then how did he know her? Was she British and here on holiday as well? She didn't look British. Suddenly Karen wondered if he'd somehow linked up with a local girl on the internet. She'd heard of it happening. It seemed unbelievable, but what else could she think? It would explain the moodiness he'd been showing as well. She choked back the tears as she wondered what to do next.

'Sorry I'm late babes, got held up'.

Steve made Karen jump as he approached her table from behind without her noticing. *He must gone round the front way*, she thought. *So that I would think he'd been in the bar watching football.* She suddenly realised that she didn't want to have it out with him here in the restaurant, with everyone watching. She had a feeling that whatever she said would make her look stupid. She decided to bide her time and gather more evidence.

'Good game was it?' She looked at him closely while she twirled her wineglass in her hand.

'Er, yeah, great. Madrid done really well.'

'I thought you said it was Barcelona?'

'Er, yeah, it was. Madrid *v.* Barcelona.'

What was the score then? One all to you? Karen thought, but checked herself. She would have to think about this a bit more.

'Come on then, let's get something to eat. You must be starving, I know I am', said Karen, as she led the way to the buffet through a crowd of screeching children.

They ate quickly and Steve announced he was tired and wanted to go to bed.

He grinned. 'Got to get a good rest before we spend all day lying around doing nothing tomorrow, eh babes?'

Karen wondered if that was all he was planning on doing. She was relieved anyway, she really wasn't in the mood for anything else tonight; she needed to clear her head and think properly about what could be going on.

'I think I'll just stay on here a bit longer – finish my wine and have a look at the book. I'm definitely going out to look at some churches tomorrow.' She pulled the art book out of her bag onto the table.

Steve frowned as he got up to go. 'That book again. Alright suit yourself, I've got plenty to keep myself occupied with while you're not around.'

Karen flushed and her voice cracked. 'Then why don't you go and do it and leave me in peace!' She turned away from him and began to flick angrily through her book.

Steve mumbled something under his breath and headed back to their room.

****

Ian entered the internet room in a state of tension. 'Internet room' was an overstatement. It was a stuffy cupboard with four antiquated yellowing computers, one of which was out of order. *Don't these people have their own laptops or iphones?* he thought. It was like something out of the early nineties. On one machine an elderly, withered woman was playing some sort of online bingo, keeping up a whispered foul mouthed commentary to herself about how the games were all fixed. Ian wondered why she bothered when there was real bingo going on in the bar. On the other, a group of boys in football clothing were surrounding the screen and blocking it from view, giggling while one of them manipulated the mouse. *Probably looking at porn*, thought Ian with disgust.

On the fourth machine two girls about 12 years old were slurping cokes and watching an inane Youtube video about a hamster on a piano. He noted with distaste that one of the girls was wearing a little cropped top with the words 'This Bitch Bites' emblazoned across the almost imperceptible adolescent swellings on her chest.

Choosing the girls as the easiest targets he stood next to them with his arms folded and said 'Going to be long?'

They ignored him. He spoke more loudly. 'I said, are you going to be long?'

This time the girls looked up. The crop top girl looked up angrily.

'Alright, alright, we was just finishing,' she said between slurps.

As they signed off Ian caught a glimpse through the door of the obese tattooed woman from before, leading her daughter in the direction of the restaurant. She saw him and scowled at him as the two girls reluctantly gave up their seats in front of the computer.

Grappling with the sticky keyboard he finally managed to get through the paywall and log on to the *Daily Defender* website. Nothing about San Itairi so far, he noticed with satisfaction. A quick scan of a couple of other major news sites showed nothing either – he was still in with a chance of an exclusive. He put his data stick in the usb port and was about to attach the file of his article to an email when the screen froze. *Not again* he thought. He began tapping the mouse button repeatedly and spoke out loud angrily. 'For fuck's sake, this is broadband, why isn't it working?'

'You mind your language, there's kids in here,' the bingo granny said with a scowl.

Ian felt like pointing out that the only kids in the room were looking at a now-frozen video clip of a woman doing something highly suspicious with a cucumber, so his language was unlikely to upset them.

The woman got up to go and turned to Ian, her expression softening a little. 'It's been happening all day. I been on at them about it but they said it's not their fault, the phone men are on strike or something, lazy sods. Keeps going on and off.'

'Did they say when it will come on again? I need to send a message urgently?'

'I don't know do I? Ask that bloke at the front desk, if you can understand him'. The woman grabbed the group of boys with a claw-like hand and they departed together, leaving Ian alone in the stifling room. He took out his data stick and hurried to the front desk.

If the telephone workers really were on strike, that was bad. Well, he corrected himself, it was good of course that the workers were asserting their rights, but didn't they realise that somebody had to get the story out about the assassination? He tapped his data stick on the desk in frustration and noticed with relief that the blowsy blonde woman in the turquoise uniform coming out of the back room. She beamed a welcoming smile at him.

'Well and how's you this evening? Everything all right with your room I hope?'

Ian wasn't in the mood for pleasantries. 'Not really, no. I'm trying to use the internet but someone said it keeps going on and off. I really need to get through to someone so I wonder if I could use your phone? I'll pay for the call of course,' he added reluctantly.

The woman seemed to look brighter than ever. 'I'm very sorry sir. At this time we have no phone or internet access usage in the hotel. I've just had a memo before the line went down that there is industrial action with the phone company for both landlines and mobiles. They're running a limited service; access will be intermittent and from time to time only until further notice, for the foreseeable future.' She clutched her clipboard and beamed at him. Ian wondered why she looked so bloody happy about it.

'Alright, thanks.' He turned to go then paused.

'Look, you will let me know if the phones and internet are back on won't you?'

'I certainly will my love, it's making my life a misery as well. You never know what you've got until you lose it, do you? So you just relax and take advantage of our facilities and don't worry, I'll let you know as soon as you can make a call.'

She disappeared into the back office and slammed the door shut, leaving a lingering smell of cheap perfume. Ian realised he was incredibly hungry and decided to risk the restaurant. He wondered what delights would be waiting for him *there*.

As he passed through the pool area he saw it was now packed with people. He noticed that several of the balconies overlooking the pool had union jack towels hung over the railings. *It makes the place look like some sort of BNP rally*, he thought with distaste. Many of the people in the crowd were noticeably drunk and talking loudly over the 'entertainment' which consisted of a lone man on the stage, wearing a Hawaiian shirt and singing something that sounded like *Una Paloma Blanca* while accompanying himself on a keyboard. Ian wondered why he even bothered playing it as it was the kind of instrument that could probably have played itself. The man was singing so close to the microphone that his voice was badly distorted and he almost shouted the word *blanca* in each chorus.

Ian lingered a moment to watch. He'd never actually seen *anything* like this before. He wondered for a moment if it was meant to be ironic and realised with horror that it wasn't. Some of the audience were even joining in with the singing, and he noticed two large women near the stage in an advanced state of excitement, making giant stirring movements with invisible spoons. Ian shuddered and hurried to the restaurant which was now mercifully almost empty.

He now suddenly realised what the point of the armband was. It was to identify hotel residents; nobody was having to pay anything or give a room number to get served at the buffet; if someone from outside had wandered in they could have got anything they wanted free of charge. *As if they'd want to,* he thought, eyeing the unappetising looking food in half empty metal trays, their contents curling up under heat lamps. Why would anyone want to gatecrash this place? Then he felt guilty as he remembered this was a poor country; a family could probably live quite well on the leavings he noticed on the empty tables, and maybe there were cases of locals trying to sneak in. *Typical multinational corporation,* he thought. Fencing themselves off from the local economy and the reality of local life.

He noticed that at this late hour most of the food was gone. It said on the door that the evening meal was from six pm, which seemed incredibly early. He and Jenny never ate before seven thirty. The place was now almost empty with only a handful of people. He noted the half-decent girl from the room next door to his sitting on her own in a corner, and wondered what had happened to the thick looking boyfriend.

The salads were all being taken away by staff so he decided on the least harmful looking option left which was lasagne with a side plate of chips. *Lasagne and chips!* He couldn't believe it. So much for his visions of a seafood dinner with a glass of wine. At least there was plenty of wine, he thought, as he sat down and a waiter offered him a glass from a big cardboard box with a spigot attached to it. *Stowells of Chelsea*, he saw on the label. He'd assumed they'd gone bust about the time *Blue Nun* had.

As the waiter moved on he heard a rough voice angrily speaking from another table. He half turned to see a fat shaven-headed man waving the wine waiter away.

'No mate, I want lager. I don't want wine.'

'I'm sorry sir. I will get you lager.'

'Cheers mate.'

Ian noted four empty pint glasses on the man's table and wondered what they'd make of all this in the Groucho Club or Soho House. He began to think about his social background in a way he hadn't really done before.

It wasn't that he was a snob, in fact far from it. He'd always been brought up to look down on snobbery as a narrow minded, middle class trait. His parents, both educationalists, had of course been staunch supporters of the comprehensive school system, but had felt that the state schools in their catchment area didn't live up to the high standards that the system ought to exemplify, so they had instead sent him to a fee-paying independent day school on the outskirts of London, called Merchant Hosiers.

It hadn't been some sort of Tory hellhole with compulsory religion, army cadets or any of that rubbish, in fact it had a reputation for being progressive, but Ian did sometimes wish he'd been to the local comp instead where things would undoubtedly have come into contact with people who were more...well...*edgy*. But then again, without Hosiers he might not have got to do Politics, Philosophy and Economics then art history at Cambridge and make the contacts that had furthered his media career. He'd been right to try for Fitzjames College. He hadn't done that well on his entrance exam, but he'd found out later that the tutor who interviewed him had liked him immediately as they shared similar political views.

Jenny was scathing of his school and university background, which she said were elitist, but he'd always thought that talented people needed to be educated a bit differently, and maybe sometimes that meant that, although he wasn't elitist himself, he had probably picked up some surface traits that might *appear* elitist. He shuddered and hoped not. He always tried to be ordinary; even called other men 'mate' and talked about football with them. But this place...it really was the limit.

He wondered if perhaps he ought to just loosen up a bit more and try to make the best of the experience. Sit back and enjoy the ride. *Anyway*, he thought to himself. *Enough of all this, I'm getting tired and brooding on things too much. Have supper and get a good night's sleep and then get home as quickly as possible.*

He began eating the flabby lasagne, and suddenly realised he was hungrier than he thought. He looked down to serve himself some chips and noted with surprise that the plate was gone. How had that happened? Had the waiter taken it away without him noticing? Then he saw a small child near his table, greedily wolfing down the chips.

'Hey, give those back!' he called out angrily without thinking.

The girl ran to the other side of the restaurant to a table and Ian followed, anger rising inside him. He realised it was the thin little girl he had noticed before and she had run to the table where her obese tattooed mother was sitting.

He stopped and suddenly wondered if he ought to be making a fuss. *But really...these people*, he thought. He realised the woman was looking at him with a furious expression.

'You got a problem?' she said, angrily.

'That girl just took my chips.' He realised he sounded like a spoilt child and wished he hadn't bothered to follow her.

The woman was not impressed by the explanation.

'Well so what? Everything's free here, ain't it?'

'That's hardly the point. I was just about to eat them.'

The girl was snivelling now, and the woman's jowls quivered with anger.

'Here. Take your chips then.' She thrust the plate at Ian who grabbed it. 'But don't you dare shout at my kid again. She does anything wrong you speak to me, not her. I swing for anyone who goes near my kid. You're just lucky my bloke ain't here.'

She looked Ian up and down with disgust. He felt like telling her a few home truths, but then remembered Jenny's rule about ignoring awkward situations in public in London. *Don't engage with them,* she always said, if there was trouble on the bus or tube, as there sometimes was. *Just turn up your music and ignore it.* Unfortunately, this was one situation where he couldn't take refuge in his gadgets. He subtly looked around and realised that shaved-head man was scowling at him also, his chip-laden fork held halfway between his plate and his open mouth, waiting to see what would happen next.

Ian held his head high and walked back in silence to his table. As he finished his meal he could hear the mother's cigarette lighter clicking rapidly and the child speaking in a loud whisper.

'Mum, who's your bloke?'

****

On the other side of the island, Miguel was deep in conversation with the four men who had arrived at his studio. Two sat with him at the table while the other two kept watch at the door and window, their hands always close to their rifles.

'We must move soon,' said one of them, poring over a large map spread out on the table. 'We know that the government fear something is going to happen. All San Itairians have been stopped from leaving by plane and we have heard that troops have begun closing off the beach, so that nobody can escape by sea. The people are reaching fever pitch. Strikes are now taking place in most of the shops, restaurants and taxi companies, and very few tourist flights are taking off.'

'No flights?' asked Miguel with a worried expression. This could cause problems with his plan.

'There are some,' replied the other man, whose name was Jose, 'but very few. Nobody seems to know which ones are taking off. Some tourists are able to leave the island but many are having to stay in the hotel.'

'Is there panic yet? Among the tourists?' asked Miguel. He wondered whether it was true that the British always kept calm in a crisis.

'No, relax, the tourists know nothing,' replied Jose. 'Even the British Embassy knows nothing.'

'That is good,' said Miguel. 'But with the communications company on strike, this is bad, how will we coordinate our plans?'

'Miguel, Miguel, with our runners we don't need telephones. They are tapped anyway, most of them. The industrial action is intended only to disrupt the government's communications. Our agents, posing as managerial staff running a skeleton service, are allowing them to work sometimes to keep essential services going and so that the government does not suspect sabotage. Once the uprising begins we will take control of them so that the world will know what is happening.'

Miguel smiled at the efficiency of his men. He realised his plan could work after all. It was time to tell them about it.

'My friends, tomorrow or the next day, we make our move. But first, before anything else, we must protect our most vital asset. If it falls into the hands of the government before we rise up, it would be a major blow to morale, as well as a huge financial loss for our cause. Jose, you say you can get the telephones to work?'

Jose nodded. '*Si*, Miguel. We can send a runner to the exchange, and we can get the 3g network online, but we will need notice.'

Miguel paused. 'Can you get the system to work by midnight, so that I can put through a call to someone on the island?'

'*Si, si,* of course. We will send a messenger. But why not just send a messenger yourself to this person? What is it about?'

'I need to speak to this man myself, and it is too dangerous to travel to meet him or write a letter. Can the government intercept mobile calls?'

Jose frowned. He was a good IT man, one of the best. Finally he shook his head. 'No, I don't think so. Landlines yes, with equipment that the Russians gave years ago, but they do not have the technology to tap mobile phones.'

Miguel sighed with relief. 'Excellent. If you can get the phones working by midnight you will do a great service to this country.'

Jose's face fell. 'Tonight will be impossible. Some time tomorrow, yes, I can do it.'

Miguel's face fell. Tomorrow might be too late for his plan, but what else could he do?

'Very well, as soon as possible. Let me know immediately when the phones are working.'

Jose smiled. 'I will do anything for San Itairi, Miguel, you know this.'

Miguel nodded, and lovingly caressed the parcel on the table in front of him. He began to explain what was going to happen.

****

Karen was still in the restaurant, on her third glass of wine, and was trying to work out what to do about Steve. She couldn't decide whether she should confront him about it, watch for further evidence, or just stop being such a silly cow and realise there was some perfectly rational explanation. But there didn't seem to be one, however hard she thought about it. She decided she would sleep on it. Things always looked better in the morning, Mum always said, and she was usually right.

The restaurant was almost empty now except for a big woman and a little girl. She looked around to see if the waiter was still there but then decided it was best not to have another glass of wine. It was time for bed, assuming she could get any sleep with all the noise going on at the pool bar. Before she turned back to collect her book she noticed a man on the other side of the room, the only other person in the room now. He was that guy from the room next door, she was sure of it. So it must have been him that had had some sort of argument just now, though she hadn't been able to make it out. She was intrigued by him and watched him, slightly drunkenly, as he strolled past her table. She pushed back a strand of hair and smiled at him. He scowled back and then a flash of recognition crossed his face.

'Hello there' said Karen.

'Oh...hello,' he replied.

He looks interesting, she thought. Slightly wild hair, trendy glasses and that kind of stubble that she liked but Steve always said was poncey. Nice jacket too, in fact all his clothes were of a kind that you didn't often see men wearing, especially not in places like this.

He moved past her but then noticed the book she was holding. He looked surprised.

'I can't believe it. Are you reading *Beyond Art*?' The man's jaw had dropped slightly as he craned to read the title of the book.

Karen looked up at him. He really was quite good looking. She smiled. 'What's the matter, don't I look clever enough?'

He looked a little flustered. 'No, no, It's just...well...I was beginning to think I was the only person here whose idea of entertainment was something other than football or bingo.'

Karen laughed. 'Don't knock bingo. My gran won five hundred quid on that once. Do you know this book then?'

'You could say that. Actually I wrote part of it'. Karen noticed a look of pride on the man's face.

'You're joking.' She'd never met anyone who'd written a book before, or even part of one.

'Not at all. I'm Ian. Ian Hurst.' He thrust out his hand and Karen took it, delicately.

Karen realised that her pulse had started racing and she that she was becoming a bit flustered.

'Really? You wrote that chapter on Corantes?'

'The very same.' Ian smiled. 'And you?'

'Sorry?' Karen looked momentarily confused.

'What's your name?'

'Oh, sorry! Karen. Karen Kay.'

'So Karen. What's your interest? Professional?'

Karen laughed and began playing with her hair. 'Me? Professional? I'm not a professional anything. I'm just doing a course on art at the WEA. My teacher said this was a good book.'

'Wise man.'

'She's a woman actually.'

'Oh...er, sorry.'

Karen began counting on her fingers. 'We've done the Old Masters, the Impressionists, something else after them...post Impressionists?'

Ian nodded.

'Now we've moved on to...erm...Contemporary Conceptualism'.

'A bit of a shock after all the chocolate box stuff.'

'All the what?'

'Rubens and Titian and all that rubbish. You're doing the real stuff now.'

Karen started to wonder if she was getting out of her depth. She wasn't used to talking about...well...anything really. And here was a real live art writer in front of her.

'Sorry I'm forgetting my manners' she said. 'Sit down, please.' She waved towards the empty chair opposite her. Ian sat down.

Karen decided to stop acting like a dizzy schoolgirl and to have a proper conversation. She took a deep breath and sat up straight.

'Yes, so as I said, we're on the Contemporary Conceptuals.'

Ian looked at her appraisingly, as if he was interviewing her for a job.

'Do you like them?'

'Oh yes, yes, I do...well...except they're a bit difficult, aren't they?'

'Difficult?' There was a note of suspicion in his voice.

'Well, I mean, I find them hard to understand.'

'That's perfectly natural. They're meant to be challenging.'

'Yes, yes I suppose so. It's just that...well...Steve, that's my boyfriend, well, fiancé actually, says it's all a load of rubbish. I want to go to some of the galleries here but he says I shouldn't. He'd rather watch the football, that's where he is now actually. I don't know anyone who likes art, really.'

A sour look momentarily crossed Ian's face. *Was it when I mentioned Steve?*, Karen wondered to herself. Ian seemed to ponder for a while then looked at her intently.

'Well, people like to mock what they can't understand. Most people think art should just be pictures of flowers and kittens. As soon as it starts challenging their preconceived political ideas, they don't want to know so they mock it. It's an instinctive conservative reaction.'

Karen wasn't sure if she followed all this. She knew some painters were political, but did that mean there were Conservative painters and Labour painters? She just wasn't sure and wished she was more clever. She noticed they were alone in the dining room and couldn't think of anything to say, so said the first thing that came into her head.

'So, enjoying your holiday then?' She realised how silly and unintellectual *that* sounded.

Ian guffawed, almost as if she'd made a joke. 'God no! I'm not on holiday. I'm working. I've just done an interview with Corantes actually.'

Karen remembered reading that Corantes lived on the island.

'Wow, that's amazing. Did you see any of his paintings? I've heard they don't show them in the galleries here, but I don't know why.'

Ian looked disgusted. 'Right wing dictatorship, the Catholic church, all the usual suspects. Hardly the place for a holiday. That's why I'm only staying here until the airport reopens.'

Of course, thought Karen. Someone who wrote books and articles on art would never go on holiday in a cheap place like this. He probably went to smart places like Italy or the south of France. She suddenly felt very...what was the word? Provincial.

'Oh yes, I heard something about the flights being interrupted. Didn't really pay much attention though,' said Karen lamely. Despite what had happened earlier, she started to wonder if she should really be sitting chatting to a strange man all alone like this.

'Well...' she smiled and stood up. Ian took the hint but seemed reluctant to leave her.

'Yes, right, good idea, got an early start tomorrow myself. Shall I walk back to your room with you?'

Karen looked doubtful and Ian must have noticed her expression.

'I mean, we're neighbours, aren't we?' he offered, hurriedly.

'Oh yes, of course, I saw you earlier,' replied Karen. 'Come on then.'

They left the dining room and walked through the pool area. The entertainment was winding down now, the last few drinkers clustered on high stools around the fake palms and coconuts by the bar. After a couple of minutes they reached their terrace.

Ian was talking away on something to do with art, or politics, or both, Karen wasn't sure which; the night air and the jet lag had hit her and made her realise she was drunker than she thought. She wondered if Steve would be asleep or if he'd see them together. *Tough luck if he does*, she thought.

Ian put his key in his door and paused. 'Well, I'll say goodbye then, as I'll be off pretty early tomorrow. I hope you, er, enjoy your holiday.'

Karen lingered on the terrace, reluctant to end what had become an interesting evening. If she was honest with herself, she also found Ian a tiny bit attractive and the sense of getting her own back on Steve was very satisfying. Suddenly she thought of something.

'Oh wait, can you sign this?' She proffered her copy of *Beyond Art* to him.

Ian laughed. 'A groupie eh? Aren't I supposed to sign your chest with a felt pen?'

They both giggled and Karen wondered if he'd moved just that little bit too close to her deliberately as he drew her to the white plastic table and opened the book, smoothing the pages down. He clicked the top of a biro.

'Now, who should I make this out to?' He began to write. 'To Karen. A rose in a bed of thorns.'

They both laughed again. Karen heard the door behind her click open and turned to see Steve emerge, wearing just his shorts and tee shirt, rubbing the sleep from his eyes as he noticed them. Ian stepped back smartly from the table.

'Oh it's you,' said Steve.

Karen recognised the grumpy tone in his voice and realised she'd better call it a night.

'Just coming in. This is my boyfriend, Steve, this is Mr Hurst.' Steve nodded at Ian curtly.

'Call me Ian, please,' insisted Ian. There was an awkward silence.

'So you were watching the football, Steve?' said Ian, in a friendly voice. Karen wasn't sure but she thought his voice had got a bit more of a London accent to it.

Steve still looked at them blankly. 'Yeah. Two nil draw. That's three points down on aggregate now. You see it as well?'

Ian looked as if he'd just missed a major event in his life. 'No, bloody missed it. I was working.'

'Oh, do you like football then Ian?' asked Karen. He didn't seem the type, somehow. 'Who do you support? Spurs or Arsenal I suppose, coming from London?'

'Sure. Well, both really, depends on who's playing.'

There was another pause. It looked like Steve was in one of his silent moods. Karen turned to go but Ian seemed to want to prove something and started talking animatedly, his voice taking on more of a London accent than ever.

'To be honest I don't like the English teams much. They're not much good, really, when you think about it. I support Brazil, really.'

Steve snorted, or did he just sniff loudly? Anyway, Karen thought it would be best to end the conversation and moved into the doorway beside Steve.

'You from Brazil, then?' asked Steve. Karen cringed. Obviously he wasn't from Brazil.

'God no. Not that there would be anything wrong with that, I mean', replied Ian, hastily. 'It's just they play the best game, don't they, the Brazil? You know, the yellow and green; pure football. Maradona, and all that. I was at one of their games in Rio recently. We had a great view from a box, and...'

Steve cut him off. 'Goodnight then mate.'

Karen caught a last glimpse of Ian still standing awkwardly on the terrace as Steve pulled the door to.

'Thanks for the book,' she called out, as Steve flicked off the light and got into bed without saying anything.

****

Pauline had had to drag Angie away from the bar. They'd been sitting in there ever since they'd finished their tea. She mentally corrected herself. *Dinner, they'd call it here*. They'd had some of those tequila things with umbrellas in them, and while she'd only had a couple, Angie must have had three or four and was starting to slur her speech and be far too loud. Anyway, the bar had closed and she'd thought it best to get back to their room. Now they'd got back to their terrace but Angie was insisting on a last fag at the table before turning in.

She noticed that young man from earlier sitting on his own at the table outside his room. He was fiddling with a laptop or computer thing of some kind, and didn't seem to notice them, so she let well alone and tried to keep her voice down. Angie was still in full flow, this time about what they'd had for their tea. Their *dinner*.

'I'm telling yer Paul. Those were leftovers heated up.' Angie's head swayed slightly as she tried to get her mouth in the right place for her cigarette.

'Well what's wrong with that? Waste not, want not. It's a poor country is this.'

Angie, as ever, wasn't in the mood for explanations.

'Look, this place is meant to be four star. You don't get leftovers in four star. Still, four star here in't the same as four star at home I suppose. And as for that wine – ugh, like battery acid. No class at all.'

The booze seemed to be making her worse, which was the opposite of what Pauline had hoped. She thought she'd best just make light of it.

'And what do you know about wines? It tasted all right to me. Gets yer drunk, that's the main thing!'

Angie didn't seem to hear.

'And the waiters don't know a thing about food. There was some stuff in a pot on the buffet, and when I asked what it was, that feller said "sauce for the meat". Turns out it were gravy! I told him sauce comes in bottles, but he didn't seem to take it in.'

'Oh Ange, he probably didn't understand a word you said, poor lad.'

Angie suddenly seemed to sober up and become more indignant than ever.

'Well I'm not satisfied. Crammed full as well, that dining room. And as for the people – talk about the tattoo and scar brigade. This place is supposed to be all exclusive.'

Pauline carried on calmly. 'It's all *in*clusive. Not *ex*clusive. Don't mean the same thing. Just means you don't pay for owt. Anyway they can't help the overcrowding. The whole place is overcrowded – everywhere is. A woman at the salad bar told me she reckons they've stopped all flights off the island. She was supposed to leave tonight but they're letting her stay on.'

Angie was livid. She stubbed her cigarette out angrily in the ashtray. 'What, for free? While we're paying?'

'I don't know do I? Probably on her insurance or summat. Anyway, it'll all come to nowt.'

She noticed the young man on the other table was looking at them.

'Come on, let's get to bed. It's past midnight. This gentleman wants to read his computer in peace.'

Angie snorted and looked over. 'Oh *him*. He never stops working, that one. Probably putting everything we say down in print.'

The young man stood up and came over. Pauline hoped he wasn't going to start complaining as well.

He stopped at their table. 'Actually I was rather interested in what you said about flights being stopped. Was there some news about the political situation?'

Pauline noticed he spoke nicely and seemed a decent sort. Perhaps he wasn't a complainer. Pauline smiled up at him. 'About the what, love?'

'The political situation – with the workers' party.'

Pauline had no idea what he was on about. 'Oh, is someone having a party?'

The man sighed and seemed a bit annoyed.

'No, no, I mean a *political* party.'

Angie looked up and struggled to focus on the man's face. 'We're not really interested in politics love, I'm afraid. I suppose you get a lot of it in London though, what with Houses of Parliament being right on your doorstep.'

The man sighed again. *Is he some sort of official?* wondered Pauline. He didn't look much like he was on holiday.

'Never mind…I just wondered if you'd heard about flights, off the island – are they still going? I'm supposed to be going back to London tomorrow. Nobody seems to know anything.'

Pauline suddenly remembered something. 'Oh, no, love – a lady from Rotherham were telling me about it in the buffet queue. They've all been stopped. Nobody's getting in or out now, they've closed the airport apparently.'

The man looked like he was about to have a heart attack.

'This is outrageous! Why wasn't I told? Did she say how long it would go on for?'

'No love, sorry – I mean, I didn't really think much of it, we're not going home for a fortnight, it'll all have blown over by then.'

He still looked upset so she thought hard for something that might console him.

'These foreign places, they're always having disputes and what not. It's the...the national character.'

'There's no such thing as "national character"' said the man angrily. He didn't seem very consoled.

Angie struggled to focus again and started to sing *Una Paloma Blanca*. Pauline thought she'd really have to get Angie to bed. This was getting ridiculous. Arguing with a stranger when they were meant to be on holiday.

'If you'll excuse me I'd like to get at least *some* sleep before I finally get out of here!' The man stalked off to his room and slammed the door.

Well, thought Pauline. *Some people.*

Angie had started to snore. Pauline shook her and was just getting her to her feet as a couple walked past to their room, speaking German. The sound roused Angie from her slumber and she raised her arm up. Pauline cringed as she realised Angie was making a Nazi salute and, to make matters worse, was starting to sing.

'Rule, Brittania...Britannia rulesa waves...'

As the Germans hurried off with horrified looks on their faces, Angie turned and blew a loud raspberry, waving a 'v' sign at them as Pauline ushered her into the room as quickly as she could.

Seven

Early the next morning, General Pedro Caudillo Del Toro stepped out of his staff car onto the shimmering tarmac of the coast road by the beach at Las Cantatas, already uncomfortably hot in the morning sun, and listlessly returned the smart salutes and heel-clickings of his aides as they ushered him over to view the newly built defensive positions.

He squinted and put his dark glasses on, allowing his eyes to relax a little. He had had a late night at the Presidential palace, talking until the early hours over brandy with the President about the possible rebel uprising. Then he had staggered into bed with one of the President's courtesans, managing to get just a couple of hours' sleep. He, as commander of the island's forces, had assured His Excellency that the military were well able to take care of any trouble, but he felt it his duty to inspect things personally; should anything go wrong, it would be his head on the block, almost literally.

He nodded admiringly as he was shown well concealed machine gun posts among the rocks by the beach, and the long lines of barbed wire fencing that had been put up by the road. If the rumoured uprising did take place, it was likely that the rebels might try to escape by sea to Cuba, where those communists (he spat on the sand at the word) were probably doing all they could to help their brothers on San Itairi. It was vital, then, that any escape route was cut off.

'Has there been any trouble with the English hotel?' asked Del Toro to the men around him.

A young lieutenant, something to do with public relations, stepped forward and clicked his heels smartly. *Public relations,* thought Del Toro with disgust. *What kind of army has this become?* Peasant conscripts from the hills and boys from the university fighting with press releases instead of guns. He longed for a good war, a chance to wipe out the scum that were trying to turn this island into the mirror image of everywhere else, with their ideas about equality and human rights.

'There has been no trouble with the hotel, sir,' flustered the young officer, as he flicked through some papers on a clipboard. 'The hotel management has been fully briefed and has assured us there will be no trouble.'

So there should not be, thought Del Toro; how many other holiday companies were privileged enough to have an entire island to themselves without competition? He frowned as he heard raised voices further along the beach. He turned to see a group of tourists, all men, wearing only shorts, their flabby chests and pot bellies burnt red. Some of their shorts and towels had the British flag on them, or that other one, the red cross only, which he thought might be the flag of Scotland.

Some of the men were jeering at the young conscripts by the barbed wire fence and *no pasar* signs but their friends were urging them away, and finally the group stalked back to the hotel, one of the men turning to shout something and make that insulting sign with two fingers instead of one.

One of the junior officers in Del Toro's party had jogged over and a few moments later came running back, slightly breathless, and saluted again.

'I am very sorry sir. Some small trouble with the British tourists. They were not happy about the beach being closed.'

'There was no violence, I hope? The soldiers did not touch them?'

'No, sir. The corporal in charge of the squad says he could not understand them but they seemed angry, and one of them started to bare his backside so the corporal pushed him away. I managed to explain the situation to them in English. They have gone back to the hotel now.'

'So I see. Tell the men they did well to restrain themselves. The British are not to be molested in any way, *comprende*? It would be a, how you say, public relations disaster for us if they were, no? He smiled at the young PR officer who smiled back, and clicked his heels.

'Indeed sir, it would. In England, at the University of East Lincolnshire where I attended my public relations degree, we learnt that...'

Del Toro cut off the enthusiastic gabbling and turned back to the car. 'Yes, yes. Carry on.'

The officers took this as the signal to get on and look busy so they began shouting orders at the conscripts nearby. In a few moments Del Toro was being driven back to the barracks in the air conditioned luxury of his staff car.

He passed the group of men who had been turned away from the beach and they caught sight of the car and began jeering and making Nazi salutes.

He caught the look of disgust on his driver's eyes in the mirror, but he chuckled to himself. He had to admire the British in a way. They just didn't care. No San Itairian would have dared to do that, as he would have known he would receive a beating, or worse. When the hotel complexes had first opened, many of the San Itairians had been shocked by the way some of the British behaved, especially the younger ones.

The San Itairians, brought up on a diet of old English serials on the state TV channel and news reports of the British royal family, had thought all English were polite gentlemen and ladies who drank tea and played croquet, not these drunken, foul-mouthed products of the English *barrios* who shouted and brawled and vomited in the streets of the Old Town. Del Toro, who avidly read history, especially military history, knew better; he knew that there was an anarchic streak in the heart of the British which was both their strength and their weakness.

The British didn't care, Del Toro had read in the Spanish translation of some dusty volume of British history, partly because they lived in a socialist society with no respect for authority, but also because they had a vicious streak in them which swung between bravery and savagery.

The British, he had read, were once fearsome in battle, especially *las Scocias*, the Scottish, who were known as the 'devils in skirts'; after all, they had defeated his own people, the colonial Spanish whose stock he came from, the Dutch, the French and finally the Germans, had conquered a quarter of the world and ruled it with the iron will of a mere handful of men. 'The scum of the earth', the great General Wellington had called his men, and Del Toro suspected that Wellington meant it as a compliment.

He wondered sadly whether those young men on the road had even heard of Wellington; from what he could tell, Britain had now gone completely soft and that social welfare and progressive thinking had weakened the country beyond repair, its citizens heedless of their country's past glories, frittering away their lives in state-funded drinking, debauchery and the breeding of *bastardos*. If that vicious streak could be properly channelled and disciplined, what a nation it would be again!

It would never happen, of course. It was a sad thought, he reflected; but then again, if the British brought money into San Itairi, then there was some good in it; and it was true, they spent like sailors on leave; and the problems they caused were largely contained in the resorts and a few streets in the Old Town. They didn't seem inclined to go anywhere where they would not meet their own kind and for that he was thankful.

He decided he would definitely go back and visit the beach again soon, to make sure there was no trouble with the British. As the car pulled into the barracks he rubbed his eyes and wondered if it was too early for a *gin tonica*.

****

Ian was woken by a blast of tinny music coming from somewhere outside his room. He sat bolt upright, for a while not realising where he was, then it all came back to him. His mouth was parched and the sheets were soaked in his sweat, the poky white room clammy and uncomfortably hot even at eight in the morning. He dimly recognised the pop song being played somewhere by the pool area. *Wheels on fire, rolling down the road...what on earth is that all about? This place is just bizarre. Still, I'll be out of here as soon as...Christ.*

He suddenly remembered what that woman had said last night. Something about there being no flights. That couldn't be right, surely? He picked up his mobile but as before, there was no signal. He made a decision: if they couldn't give him a straight answer at reception he would go to the airport himself. He decided he'd rather sleep on the terminal floor than stay a moment longer in the hotel.

After a quick shower he rapidly packed his bag and walked briskly through the pool area. A group of elderly people were queuing at a little hut by the pool to collect sun loungers, and his stomach lurched as he smelt bacon, eggs and rancid cooking fat wafting from the dining room. Well, he wasn't staying for any more of that muck. A croissant and coffee at the airport would be enough, assuming the airport had such a thing as a Costa. Even a Starbucks would be good enough.

At reception, he plonked his key on the desk, thinking this must be one of the last hotels in the world to not use key cards. There was nobody about in the lobby or behind the desk. The hotel seemed much quieter this morning. He wondered about pinging the big brass bell but thought that might look a little too middle-class and arrogant, so he settled for a loud cough instead. Nobody came. He looked at his phone; plenty of time before the one o'clock flight. *If* it was running, he thought glumly.

He suddenly realised that someone was standing close to him at the desk. He turned and saw the obese woman he'd argued with in the canteen the night before. As usual she had her little girl in tow. He turned away but felt a podgy finger on his sleeve. What the bloody hell did she want now?

He looked at her and saw her smiling, almost leering at him.

'Listen, about last night. Lianne's got something to say to you.' She pushed her daughter forward.

There was a moment of silence as Ian stared at the thin little girl who was looking down at the ground and twisting her foot in awkwardness.

The obese woman nudged her. 'Come on, ain't you got something to say to the man?'

Ian heard the girl mumble. 'Sorry I took your chips.'

The woman nudged her again. 'Say it properly.'

The girl looked up at Ian and said 'Sorry I took your chips mister, I won't do it again.'

Ian sighed with relief and tried to smile. 'That's fine, don't worry about it, seriously.'

The woman smiled again but stopped as they turned to go. Her manner had softened considerably and Ian almost felt sorry for her.

'Yeah right, listen, sorry if I was a bit rude and that. It's just, well, you know, 'cos you were on your own and didn't have no wife and kids with you, I just thought, well...'

What on earth is she on about? thought Ian. The woman continued. 'Can't be too careful can you, with kids around, not with all them things you hear about nowadays.'

Then he realised with horror what she was driving at. *She* actually *thought I was a child molester! Sweet Jesus, was there no end to the ignorance of these people?*

The woman was still talking. 'But then I saw you with your girlfriend and realised you was ok.'

Ian's brain whirled in confusion. Girlfriend? But Jenny was back home in London and...he suddenly realised she must mean that woman from the room next door, what was her name? Karen. He was about to set the woman right when he suddenly stopped. Perhaps it was best to say nothing.

'Bye then' said the woman, waddling away with the little girl.

This place is like a bad dream, thought Ian. *It's like a holiday thought up by Kafka.* God only knew what would have happened in a place like this had rumours circulated that he was a child molester. He was suddenly keen to get shot of this place as quickly as possible.

Then he caught a whiff of cheap perfume and the rep woman, Trisha, appeared. Cutting her off to avoid wasting time he quickly said 'I'm checking out, I've got a flight at one. Can you get me a taxi as well?'

Trisha's smile faltered a little but she soon regained her composure.

'Oh dear, sorry you're leaving us. I hope you've had a nice time at this time?'

'Yes, great, but I don't want to miss my flight, so if you could just....'

'Certainly sir, no problem at all, let me just check you out.'

Ian tapped his fingers on the reception desk impatiently as Trisha took a long time looking at the computer screen.

'Now as I said before, we have only had sporadic internet access from time to time, but I have been able to find out and ascertain that we are having rather a problem with the flights today.'

'What do you mean, rather a problem?'

'It's nothing to be concerned about at this point in time, but we are having a few small major delays due to the industrial action at the airport.'

A few small major delays? What does that even mean, thought Ian. Couldn't this woman speak English?

'Can you get me on the flight or not?'

Trisha smiled brightly. 'We will endeavour to try to do our utmost best to get you on your scheduled flight, but please be aware that we are experiencing quite a backlog and currently the transfer coaches are unavailable, so I suggest that...'

Ian had had enough. He slammed his room key on the desk and stalked out into the dazzling sunlight, hoping to grab a taxi on the main road at the end of the long, dusty hotel driveway.

****

Three hours later he was back in the hotel, exhausted. After a struggle to get a taxi (it seemed most of them were on strike) it had taken an hour to drive the five miles to the airport, as military trucks jostled with buses in a long queue to enter the car park. It looked as if a lot of the Las Cantatas residents were on the hotel buses – he was sure he recognised a few of the horrors he'd seen lounging around the pool.

When he finally got into the terminal building it was like some medieval vision of hell – stifling heat and crowds of red-faced holidaymakers sprawled on piles of luggage, babies howling and the air thick with cigarette smoke. Ian noticed with distaste that they didn't even seem to have a smoking ban as he looked around for the check-in queue.

He then realised with horror that the shambolic crowd of people *was* the queue, filling the entire building like a tightly coiled rope, with heavily armed soldiers eyeing them sullenly. The information screens just showed a list of flights to various provincial British airports with 'cancelled' beside all of them.

After an hour he finally managed to locate a harassed Solarflair employee who told him that his flight would be delayed until at least tomorrow afternoon. Ian checked again to confirm what he already knew; that no other hotels on the island were available. Dismissing his previous idea of bedding down in the airport with a snort of derision, he marched out of the terminal and this time had no trouble getting a taxi. The driver eyed him with a puzzled expression when he asked to be taken back to the hotel. He swore never, never again to travel anywhere unless it was at least business class and from a *proper* airport.

Eight

Karen and Steve sat in silence in the restaurant, finishing a late breakfast. Karen had decided, whether Steve liked it or not, that she was going to go to one of the art galleries in San Itairi town.

She stirred her coffee nonchalantly. 'I thought I'd visit that art gallery today, the one up in town. Like to come?'

'Think I'll pass' muttered Steve, looking down and fiddling with his phone.

Surprise surprise, thought Karen.

'Got any reception?' asked Karen, secretly wondering what he was so interested in.

Steve looked up. 'No, it hasn't been working for ages. Last message I got was that one from...' He paused. 'Last message I got was ages ago.'

He's definitely up to something, thought Karen. *And I'm going to find out what.*

Karen got up and collected her bag. 'Right then, I'm off to the gallery. It's only a short walk. See you about oneish then.'

Steve didn't look up from his phone. 'Right, yeah, see you.'

Karen strode out of the restaurant with a look of resolve on her face. There was no going back now. She was going to find out what he was doing and if that meant she was becoming some sort of stalker (*can you stalk your own boyfriend,* she wondered) then so be it. She wasn't going to get married to some man who was having a bit on the side.

Instead of leaving the hotel she went into the loos by the dining room and put on her sunglasses and a new cardie that Steve hadn't seen before. She then took out an anonymous carrier bag from her handbag and popped her handbag in it. Not exactly an amazing disguise, but it might make it less obvious that she was following Steve. *You're really cracking up, darling,* said a small voice in her head. *But if he's seeing another woman you* have *to know about it'* said another small voice.

She checked the coast was clear outside the loos then peeped into the dining room, stepping back quickly into the shadows as she saw Steve striding towards her. She followed him at a safe distance. Instead of turning down the path to their room, he went in the opposite direction to another block of rooms, nipping up the outside stairs with a spring in his step.

Karen hid behind a wilting palm tree and watched as he made his way along the first floor terrace of the block to a room at the end. He knocked on the door and it opened. Karen felt a wave of nausea crash on her stomach as she realised who was standing in the shadowy doorway – it was the dark, attractive girl from the night before. She smiled and said something inaudible but then she heard Steve's louder voice.

'No, she's gone out. Won't be back for ages so don't worry.'

He walked in, closing the door behind him. Karen turned and ran back to her room, nodding briefly to Pauline and Angie outside the room, glad that her sunglasses hid her raw, stinging tears.

****

Trisha's day was getting worse and worse. The phones and internet were still only working occasionally and she'd just had a visit from a harassed member of staff from the British Embassy saying that they should be prepared to evacuate the hotel at short notice should the political situation in the country get worse. They were to stand by and await further orders. All very dramatic! She wondered vaguely what the political situation in the country was. It had never seemed the sort of place where you got trouble; in fact there always seemed to be a lot of police and soldiers about keeping an eye on things. She did think something must be up though as soldiers had closed the beach off and she'd had to deal with a few complaints about that. At least they'd managed to clear the backlog of residents going to the airport and they weren't letting any more flights land so that meant less work for her. She supposed it would all blow over in a few days anyway.

She looked up in surprise as the reception doors opened and Ian walked in. That was one problem she'd hoped she'd managed to get rid of. She steeled herself and put on her best smile.

'Hello stranger, and how's yourself? I thought you were on the one o'clock flight?'

Ian didn't look in the mood for conversation at all.

'So did I' he replied angrily. 'It seems I have to be here another night so I wonder if you could do whatever you have to do to get me another night in this wonderful hotel, as it is apparently beyond the ability of your company to get me away from this place until tomorrow and I have an urgent report to make'.

So he was an inspector, she thought. That woman had been right about him making out a report. He sounded really angry, thought Trisha. If he was an inspector this was about the worst thing that could happen. She would have to really turn on the Trisha charm for this one.

She hurriedly tapped some details into the computer, inwardly giving thanks that the sporadic internet service was working at that moment.

'Yes I can confirm that your room is still available and your flight has been rescheduled for 1pm in the afternoon tomorrow subject to there being no more further delays'.

Ian sighed with relief and stalked off with his room key without thanking her.

Trisha actually hoped that something serious might kick off now. He could hardly complain if there was some sort of revolution and everyone had to be evacuated. If she played her cards right she might even get a commendation. But there was still a risk he might cause trouble. She rather liked the way he looked when he was angry. She decided that she was going go nuclear on the old Trisha charm – and make sure he got something to take his mind off complaining.

****

After a very late breakfast, Pauline and Angie had settled down on the loungers outside their room. Pauline had got stuck into her paperback, Angie was dozing in the sun and it all seemed peaceful. Pauline looked around her. That young man, Ian, was outside his room fiddling with his computer as usual. That girl, Karen, had gone into her room but there didn't seem to be any sign of her young man. *Ah well*, she thought. *At least it's quiet for a bit; there seem to be fewer people in the hotel today and Angie's found nothing more to complain about.*

She jumped as Angie sat bolt upright and whipped off her sunglasses, fixing Pauline with a fierce glare. Angie's heart sank. *Spoke too soon*, she thought dismally.

'What about them Germans in the breakfast queue?' she barked loudly.

'What about them?' sighed Pauline. She noticed that Ian had stopped looking at his computer and was glaring at them.

'That dining room was full of Germans. Full of them! This is supposed to be a British hotel. I don't want foreigners around when I'm abroad, thank you very much. This place is supposed to be all exclusive.'

Pauline felt her face redden and she was sure she heard Ian mutter something under his breath. Angie didn't seem to notice and kept on talking.

'I gave them a piece of my mind actually.'

Pauline resigned herself to this new wave of complaints. 'What for?'

'For pushing in at the breakfast buffet. I told one of them, that big red German, to get back in his place, but it was like I was speaking a foreign language'.

Pauline heard Ian snort with laughter.

'Well you were, to him' he said.

Angie flashed an angry look at him. 'Don't be daft. They all understand English. He were just pretending not to.'

Pauline cringed with embarrassment as Ian got up and walked over. He looked really angry.

'Why do the British have this arrogant assumption that everyone speaks their language?'

Pauline decided to try to smooth things over. 'Well I think we should all just get along.'

Angie sniffed. 'Just get along? They don't know the meaning of the word. What would have happened in the war if we'd all just tried to 'get along' with the Germans?

'It probably wouldn't have started in the first place.' said Ian, sitting back down and fiddling with his computer again.

'Anyway, that breakfast was rotten. How do you think they cooked them sausages?' Angie was off again, but Pauline noted with relief that Ian was ignoring them.

'I don't know. Fried them I suppose. They tasted alright to me' Pauline said. She had never been much of a gourmet.

'Don't be daft. Microwaved, they were. That's why they looked like big grey dog turds.'

'Oh thanks Ange. That's helped my digestion that has' said Pauline, trying to make light of the situation. She tried to change the subject during the brief pause in conversation while Angie lit a cigarette.

'Turned out nice again,' she said brightly, looking up at the sky.

Angie sighed. 'Pauline, you said that every day on holiday last year. Of course it's turned out nice again. That's why we go on holiday. You don't get bad weather abroad.'

Pauline considered for a moment. 'They do get bad weather sometimes. What about that tsunami thing in Thailand?'

Angie tutted. 'That wasn't bad weather, that was a big wave.'

Pauline shuddered a little at the thought of it and decided to change the subject again.

'Hey, I heard from someone at breakfast that they've closed off the beach. A whole lot of soldiers turned up and put barbed wire up and they're not letting anybody on it.'

That got Ian's attention, she noticed. Angie also seemed concerned.

'Disgusting. Cooping us all up in here. Right, that's another star rating gone from this place when I do my review.'

Pauline looked puzzled. 'But you don't like beaches anyway, Pauline. You said they're always mucky.'

'They are. But that's not the point. Just because I don't like them doesn't mean they can stop me using them.'

Ian came over again. Pauline noticed he had started to look a bit excited.

'That's pretty worrying if they've closed the beach off. Flights delayed, troops everywhere, this could be the start of something big.'

He had a funny look in his eyes, thought Pauline.

Angie snorted. 'Rubbish. It'll all blow over. These countries are always kicking off over nowt. It's the hot weather that does it. The lacking temperament, they call it.'

Ian looked angry again. 'It's *latin* temperament, actually, if you must start cultural stereotyping'.

Angie laughed derisively. 'Oh, he's talking latin now! You mark my words, it'll come to nothing. It'll be like Cyprus in the seventies. That blew over as well.'

Ian exhaled sharply. 'What do you mean? It didn't "blow over" as you put it. Cyprus has been a disputed territory for decades.'

Angie was resolute. 'No it isn't. People have been going on holiday there for ages. They know what's good for them and they won't risk owt happening to the tourists. So there.'

Angie made it clear that no further conversation was wanted, and put her dark glasses back on. Pauline breathed a sigh of relief.

Ian got up and walked over to the perimeter wall. 'I'm going to see if what she says is right.' He stood on tiptoe and looked over the white concrete to the expanse of beach below.

'Bloody HELL' he shouted, then raced to the table for his camera.

****

In a network of caves deep beneath the pine forests of northern San Itairi, Miguel addressed the motley assortment of rebel leaders now under his command. He scanned the group of some twenty partisans, all friends he would trust with his life, who would soon go back to their towns and villages to mobilise the people's army that would, once and for all, free his island from fascism. This is what he had been waiting for for years; this was *his* time. He took a deep breath and paused before speaking.

'Comrades. Brothers. For years we have been secretly raising an army of revolution. You have honoured me by allowing me to be your leader. It is not a position I am worthy of'.

There was a murmur of dissent but Miguel raised his hand for silence.

'No, I am not worthy of it. I, a simple artist. A peasant, who daubs paintings; not a great general or a great leader. But for the sake of San Itairi, this land I love, I have agreed to do it.'

There was a loud cheer and Miguel waited for it to die down before continuing.

'But however careful we have been, the forces of oppression have somehow found out rumours of our planned revolution. We do not think they know everything, but we know that they know something is going on. Therefore we must strike, and strike now!' He raised his Kalashnikov in the air and the cheers rang around the caves for several minutes.

As the leaders departed for their respective villages, Miguel made final checks to maps and weapons and called over Jose, the telecommunications expert.

'*Si*, Miguel?' asked Jose, his admiration for his leader even greater after such a rousing speech.

'My friend, are the telephone workers still on strike?'

'*Si* Miguel, the lines are down almost everywhere and the government forces are only able to communicate by radio. But I will be in San Itairi town today and will be able to get the mobile phone network working briefly this afternoon, as I promised.'

Miguel smiled and clapped his hand on Jose's back. Jose involuntarily stiffened a little, remembering the reputation Miguel had. 'Jose, you are a great man. When this is over I will make you my *Ministero de Communicaciones.*'

Jose beamed with delight. Miguel frowned and drew out a large parcel from beneath a tarpaulin in a corner of the cave.

'But when you have done this, there is one further job. For this, I must trust you with my life.'

Jose swelled with pride. 'You can trust me with your life a thousand times. Tell me what I must do.'

Miguel smiled and carefully placed the bulky parcel into Jose's outstretched hands. Jose craned his neck awkwardly in order to continue looking at Miguel.

'You are to take this to the Hotel Las Cantatas today and deliver it to a man. An Englishman, named Hurst. But nobody is to see you. You must not be seen or discovered. If you are found, you must destroy the parcel with this.'

Jose gulped as Miguel gave him a hand grenade. He hugged it closely to himself, balancing it and the awkwardly shaped parcel with difficulty.

'But Miguel, if I destroy the parcel with this *bomba* surely I will kill myself also?' asked Jose in a worried voice.

Miguel smiled. 'You are a fast learner, Jose. Now, go.'

Nine

General Del Toro, despite being swathed in the cool luxury of his air conditioned staff car, was becoming annoyed. More and more rumours of an imminent rebel uprising had been coming from the *barrios* and villages. His Excellency the President was beginning to be highly concerned; he had even warned the British and German embassies of the possible uprising and now plans were being put into place to evacuate the holidaymakers should violence break out.

Del Toro saw this as a personal slight – His Excellency did not trust him to crush these filthy Marxists swiftly and discretely, causing no more upset to the tourists than if he were to crush a bug under his swagger stick. To illustrate the point he took his stick and swatted a fly on the windowsill next to him. He tutted angrily as it made a bloody mess on the cream leather interior of the door.

He was spending the day touring the island's defences and inspecting his troops to ensure that everything was ready to respond immediately to any uprising. Conscious of the fact that tourism was the island's biggest money-spinner he decided to return to the beach at Las Cantatas to ensure that disruption to the foreign tourists was at a minimum. He didn't trust those *peons* to run a brothel, let alone a machine gun emplacement.

They had arrived at the beach road. Del Toro's driver opened the door and the general stepped out onto the blazing sand to meet the officer in charge. Heels clicked and rifles clattered as the men on the beach presented arms.

Del Toro surveyed the barbed wire defences and sentry points along the shoreline with approval. Suddenly there was an outbreak of shouting, in both Spanish and English, further up the beach where the foreign hotel was located. A group of fat, shaven headed English men were jostling, shouting and laughing at each other close to the barbed wire fence.

Del Toro snapped at the officer in charge of the beach.

'What is happening? Why are these tourists here? The hotel has received strict instructions that no tourists are to go on the beach.'

The officer stammered an explanation. 'Sir, we cannot stop them, they have been coming and laughing at us all day. Will you give the order for us to fire?

Del Toro was enraged. 'No I will not! These are unarmed civilians. Where do you think you are, Africa? Call the police and have these men sent back to the hotel or arrested.'

The officer gabbled orders into his radio. There was a burst of static and then a squawking voice from the radio. The officer listened intently.

'What is he saying?' demanded Del Toro.

'He says a police vehicle of plain clothes men are in the vicinity and are coming now.'

Del Toro sighed. 'Hmm. Well, uniformed men would have been better but at least it is something. We have no power of arrest over these people. Let the *policia* sort it out.'

He turned and saw a dark four wheel drive with blacked out windows, the kind the hated secret police used, bumping its way along the beach to the small group of tourists. Then he heard more shouts and laughter. He squinted against the harsh sunlight and looked at the men, almost unable to believe what he was seeing. One of the tourists had taken off all his clothes and vaulted the barbed wire fence, running like a crazed animal towards the shoreline.

****

Ian grabbed his camera got back to the wall just in time to see the streaker leap over the barbed wire fence and run for his life down the beach, his obscene beer gut wobbling over, and mercifully concealing, his genitals. He spun and hurled away the tiny thong he had been wearing, like a stripper throwing her underwear from the stage. Ian blinked in disbelief as he focused the SLR on the man and took pictures. The man's friends jeered and laughed. He could hear them shouting in unison:

'You fat bastard! You fat bastard!'

They then started to chant a raucous song to the tune of *Ay Ay Conga*.

'*Rollo is a fat* —

Rollo is a fat —

La la la la, la la la la!'

He must be insane, thought Ian. He saw two soldiers running awkwardly across the sand towards the man, unslinging their rifles and shouting in Spanish. Then a 4x4 jeep with blacked out windows pulled up and four sinister looking men in dark glasses and casual clothing leapt out, coralling the man like farmers trying to catch an angry bullock.

By now Pauline and Angie were looking over the wall and Karen had come out of her room too.

Pauline was calling out excitedly. 'Oh my god, what's he doing? They'll kill him!'

The men from the jeep had wrestled the fat man to the ground and Ian looked on in horror as they punched and kicked him until he stopped moving.

Angie had managed to get the camera on her phone working and was taking pictures of the chaotic scene. She was screaming out at the top of her voice like some deranged granny at a wrestling match.

'You let him alone you bloody bullies! Dirty dago bastards!'

Ian started to wonder if he was dreaming all this. Did anybody use the word 'dago' anymore? He blinked and took some more pictures of the man. Then a thought struck him and he smiled grimly. *This is going all the way to the top*, he thought. *The UN, Amnesty, they're all going to get a copy of these pictures. That stupid fat idiot doesn't know what a big favour he's just done me...and western democracy. Once people see what really goes on here the regime will be out on its arse.*

Within seconds it was all over. Ian saw that the naked man, dazed and with blood pouring from his head, had been bundled into the arms of his friends. The policemen had jumped back into the jeep and sped off in the direction of San Itairi town. The soldiers on the beach, including some tin-pot general in dark glasses, had herded the men's friends up the steep steps and back into the hotel. They then pulled the barbed wire barriers up close to the staircase so that the beach was completely closed off.

An excited crowd of English tourists surrounded the men as they entered the hotel compound. Some of them turned to jeer and make obscene gestures at the remaining soldiers by the entrance but there were general calls of 'leave it' and 'they're not worth it'.

The fat man was plonked down on a lounger and a union jack towel put over his nether regions. He seemed to come out of his daze and sheepishly raised his fists in the air like a victorious boxer as his friends clapped him on the back.

Ian pushed his way through the gaggle of onlookers and took pictures of the man, alternating between crouching and standing positions.

One of the fat man's friends laughed and said 'watch out Rollo, this bloke fancies you!'

Ian, unsmiling, stood up. 'No, no, I'm a journalist.'

He fumbled to switch on his iphone recorder. 'What was that all about? Were you protesting against the beach being closed?'

He thought it unlikely that the man was much into politics, but the whole thing was beginning to puzzle him.

Karen had brought a damp cloth from her room and gave it to Rollo to press to the wound on his forehead while Pauline dabbed at the blood on his chest with her hankie. Somebody fetched a rep with a first aid case but Rollo waved them away. He laughed and sucked deeply on a cigarette that someone had lit for him and popped into his mouth.

'You really a journalist mate?' he asked Ian.

Ian nodded. 'Yes...mate. For the *Daily Defender*. Listen, this is a big story. I need to know your views on the regime, why you were protesting.'

This time Rollo and all his friends laughed. 'Views on what? I weren't protesting against nothing. I do this every year, don't I lads?'

He looked round to his friends who nodded. One rat faced man pushed himself forward.

'Yeah, he does this every year. Every time we go on holiday he has to do a streak down the beach. Sort of tradition, innit?'

Rollo puffed victoriously on his cigarette. Seeing that the man was not seriously hurt, the crowd had begun to disperse a little. 'Yeah, that's right. I done a streak on holiday every year for the last five years.'

Ian was incredulous. 'But what about the barbed wire, the armed guards? You could have been seriously injured, even killed?'

Rollo guffawed. 'Come off it mate! They wouldn't kill a tourist would they?'

'And your tackle's so tiny that barbed wire couldn't reach it anyway!' shouted the rat-faced man.

There was general hilarity and Rollo nodded approvingly. 'I done worse in Greece during the World Cup and got done over by the coppers much worse than down there. This lot were a bunch of poofs. Probably wanted to give me one in that jeep. It was only that army bloke what talked them out of it. Still, can't blame them, everybody wants my body don't they gels?'

He thrust his hips forward in an obscene gesture, the towel threatening to fall off at any moment. The few remaining women in the crowd laughed good-naturedly as they drifted away, the novelty of the event having worn off.

Rollo winced in pain as he got up. 'Come on then lads. Let's have a few beers to celebrate.' A huge cheer went up as Rollo began to limp towards the bar.

Ian couldn't believe it. He hurried after Rollo.

'But aren't you going to press charges? We need to inform the Embassy.'

Rollo looked genuinely puzzled, a look of confusion mingling with the look of bovine good nature on his face.

'Press what? Come off it mate, I'm on holiday. Good piss up, good punch up – result, innit?'

The thin faced man turned and laughed. 'Yeah, do the crime, do the time, innit? That's philosophy, that is. Stick that in your paper!'

Ian had to go and sit down for a bit. He simply could not believe that the man would let the authorities get away with that. Well, if 'Rollo' wouldn't do anything about it, then *he* would.

As he went to download his pictures onto his laptop and try to get a connection, he noticed Angie intently pressing keys on her phone.

****

Del Toro, in his staff car on the way back to headquarters, had finally calmed down after his run-in with the secret police. There had long been rivalry between them and the army over who was more loyal to the President. Del Toro didn't trust the police – they were slick city men; middle class meritocrats who spent their time with computers and files. Most of them would not last five minutes on an assault course or a field exercise.

So when they had beaten the English tourist and tried to bundle him into their jeep to do God knew what to him in the state prison, Del Toro had furiously raged at them, telling them that this could cause an international incident and ruin the island's economy. Quavering under his wrath, they had released the man and scuttled off, probably to check their hair and manicures, thought Del Toro.

He had to admit he had been impressed by the fat man. To run naked and vault a barbed wire fence with armed men around him, then get up and walk after such a beating with a grin on his face. He didn't imagine for one minute the man had consciously thought about his actions. It had been a drunken prank, but that was the point – this was the wild anarchic streak of the English. In the present days, it was wasted and directionless, but when properly drilled and disciplined, it had once subdued a quarter of the world. Del Toro shuddered to think what that man could do with a bayonet.

If, he thought, *if by some miracle the suspected uprising is successful, then I will move to England.* There would be nothing left for him here and he would be lucky to escape with his life if the rebels managed to seize power.

False papers would be easy enough to obtain, and anyway he had heard that the English allowed anybody to enter their country. Perhaps he could even join their *policia*...no, he remembered, they were unarmed. Their army, then. What a privilege it would be to command such as the fat man the next time the English invaded some god-forsaken country!

He would speak to that young officer, what was his name? The public relations man. He would get him to send the fat man a crate of champagne, *no, beer would be better*, he thought, and one of the best whores on the island, as an apology for the conduct of the police. That would ensure that no complaints were made.

As the car pulled into the barracks he started to daydream about the possibility of moving to England. He began to practice to himself some of the English phrases he remembered from old TV programmes. He imagined himself taking tea with an English lord or lady. He twiddled his little finger in the air. Was it done to raise it like so, while drinking the tea? He wasn't sure. He cleared his throat and began to recite.

'Howa do you-a do?'

'HOW ado a you ado?'

'How akind of ayou to let a me come!'

****

After all the excitement Karen had gone back to her room and rinsed out the towel she'd given to Rollo. There was no sign of Steve. She sat on the bed and tried to weigh up the evidence against Steve. *There you go again, said the voice in her head. Evidence? What do you think this is,* Silent Witness? *Don't be stupid,* said another voice. *He's playing away and you know it.*

She counted on her fingers all the warning signs she'd seen. One, he'd been distant and snappy with her the last few weeks. Two, he'd had a mystery call from someone named Anna. Three, he'd sneaked off to meet another woman twice, even going into a room with her. He might still be with her now for all she knew; they could be...she shut the image out of her head and took a deep breath. She decided she would confront him as soon as he came back. She checked her phone but there was still no signal; she wished she could have phoned mum or one of her friends to ask what to do. But this time, she was on her own.

She lay on the bed staring at the ceiling and occasionally trying to read her art book, but it was no use. Visions of cancelling the wedding and having to tell everyone they'd split up kept flashing into her brain. After what seemed an eternity she heard the door open and Steve came in, whistling under his breath.

'Hello babes'.

He leant over to kiss her but she pushed him away. A look of confusion spread across his face then he looked alarmed.

'Uh-oh. What have I done?'

'You tell me.'

'What's that supposed to mean?'

'It means where have you been this last forty minutes?'

Steve paused. 'Where have you been yourself? Thought you were going to a gallery?'

'I decided not to go. But I'm asking where you were.'

'I...just been having a walk. Round the hotel. Stretching my legs, like.'

'Oh really? So you saw all the excitement outside then?'

'Excitement?'

'That kid that fell in the pool.'

'Oh yeah, that. Saw some of it. Shocking.'

'No you didn't Steve, because it never happened. A fat guy did a streak down the beach, that's what happened, but you never saw that either did you?'

Steve looked so confused that Karen felt a pang of pity. *You are now officially in mad cow territory,* said the voice in her head. *If he dumps you you'll have deserved it, the way you're treating him.* She softened slightly, feeling the tears welling in her eyes.

'What are you doing Steve? Just tell me, yeah? I'd like to know. Who's Anna?'

Steve swallowed.

'Listen babes...I can explain...but just give me a couple of hours first, yeah?'

'Why can't you tell me now?' Karen felt a rising note of anger in her voice.

'I just can't, you'll understand later.'

He tried to smile and leant in to kiss her again but this time, Karen had had enough. What would change in two hours? He didn't even have the guts to tell her. She jumped off the bed and stalked into the bathroom, slamming the door behind her.

Ten

Later that afternoon, as the hotel's few remaining guests slumbered in their rooms in the stifling heat, or sitting idly by the pool, Ian was on the terrace working feverishly to complete his news item on the beating of Rollo. He'd got his camera card in his laptop and had chosen the best pictures and was making the final touches to his copy, working in the stuff about the assassination of the opposition leader as well. He'd been to the internet room but there was still no online access and every few minutes he tried to get connected via his laptop. The line *had* to work soon. He carried on typing.

In a graphic example of the brutality of Felipe Rivera's fascistic regime, a British tourist was stripped and beaten senseless today by police after taking an innocent stroll on the beach.

Ian smiled. Not quite accurate of course, but it sounded better than 'drunken thug gets what he deserves for idiotic prank.'

The man, who does not wish to be identified, was too traumatised to comment...

He looked up as Angie and Pauline stepped out on to the terrace. *Not them again*, thought Ian, keeping his head down and trying to get on with his work.

Angie was looking intently at her phone. 'I think it's working now Paul.'

Pauline smiled wanly. 'Oh that's nice Ange. Maybe he'll call you back now like he said.'

Ian looked up, his full attention now focused on the two women.

'Hey, are the phones working?' he asked, excitedly. Just then Angie's mobile trilled and she pressed the answer button, making shushing gestures to Ian.

'Hello, hello, can you hear me?' Angie spoke in a loud, slow voice with the genteel inflection she'd used earlier with Ian.

Without hesitating Ian clicked on the necessary buttons to get internet access on his laptop. Then he stopped as he heard the conversation between Angie and the caller.

'Yes, yes this is Mrs Angie Belper. To whom am I speaking to? *Sun* news desk?'

Ian's mouth dropped open in horror. Was she speaking to a journalist? He got up and strode over, clicking his fingers and making gestures for her to give him the phone. Angie glared at him and turned away.

'Yes, yes, I'm here. Did you get them photos I sent you of that lad? You did, good. And you want to do an article on it? Yes, I'm happy to comment.'

Ian made another grab for the phone and hissed at Angie. 'Let me handle this, I'm a journalist for God's sake. I need to speak to them'.

This time Pauline stepped between them. She flashed an angry look at Ian, which he noticed was a change from her usual meek expression. 'You leave her alone. She's trying to report the policemen that did over that lad. Use your own phone if you want to call someone.'

Ian stepped back in frustration. How could he explain to these stupid women that the story needed to be professionally reported in an objective manner?

Angie had lit a cigarette and was getting into her stride. 'Yes that's to whom I want to speak to. I called earlier and you were going to call me back as I'm not paying owt for this call. Yes, yes he was beaten up something terrible. Me and my friend, that's Mrs Pauline Beswick...B...E...S... yes, that's right, well anyway, we saw the whole thing. That poor lad was just having a laugh and some fellers put the boot in. Yes, them ones in the picture.'

Ian decided it was a lost cause and sat down at his laptop, sticking in the USB stick he'd used in the internet room to check some last minute details on his previous article on the assassination. Then he stopped, unable to believe what he was hearing as Angie prattled on.

'Well I don't know who they were. No, they weren't soldiers. I don't think they were coppers either. No, just ordinary blokes, no uniforms. That's right. Communist rebels? I'm not sure. Are there any on this island? Oh I see. Well, I suppose they must have been then if they weren't in uniform.'

'No, no!' hissed Ian, rushing over to Angie. 'Give me that phone, they'll get the whole story wrong. It was the fascists, not communists!'

This time Angie was resolute. She spoke brightly to the man on the phone. 'Would you excuse me a minute please. Thank you.' She then glared at Ian.

'Look you. I've had enough of this. You mind your own business and get back to your computer.' She jabbed a finger at his laptop. 'Looks like it's gone all funny anyway. I'd check on that if I were you.'

Ian looked over at his laptop, his eyes widening in surprise, as Angie continued to speak on the phone. The screen looked as if it were slowly melting, and a red warning box flashed angrily. Ian leant over the table and felt an icy chill as he read the words in the box.

'Trojan X34t virus alert. All systems disabled.'

In a panic he started clicking keys and rubbing the mouse pad wildly, but nothing seemed to work. He realised he must have caught a virus from using his usb stick in the internet room. He tried to keep calm and concentrate on saving his data but kept being distracted by Angie talking on the phone.

'Right then. Yes, so them communist rebels beat up that feller, and it was only some army bloke what saved him. Yes, a general or something. He sent them rebels packing and got the bloke back into the hotel. He seemed like a decent sort...'

Ian desperately rebooted his computer, then slumped in the white plastic chair as he discovered all his picture files were gone – Miguel's painting, the assassination, the beating on the beach. All wiped. His articles had gone too. He slammed the lid of his laptop closed, and glared in fury at Angie, who had hung up and was now sitting down and lighting another cigarette. God only knew what sort of misinformation a paper like that would give out. Beaten to a scoop, by the *Sun*, of all bloody papers!

She laughed. 'See, anyone can be a journalist! They're putting that on their website right away, he just told me. And I get fifty quid for it, it says here!' She brandished a four day old copy of the tabloid with an advertisement that read *Got a story? Call our newsline now. £50 for all stories published.*

Angie stood up. 'Come on Pauline. I feel in a good mood. Let's have one of them drinks with umbrellas to celebrate.'

Pauline smiled and they both walked off in the direction of the pool bar.

We'll see about that, thought Ian as he checked his own mobile, which was now showing a signal. *Nobody reads those tabloids anyway*, he thought. *Well, nobody who counts.* He would phone his office and dictate the real story straight away.

Before he had a chance to dial, the phone rang and he jumped as he felt it vibrate in his hand. He didn't recognise the number. He tentatively pressed 'accept' and put the phone to his ear.

'Hello, Ian Hurst speaking?'

It was Miguel.

****

A few minutes earlier, Jose had smiled as he left the telecommunications building in San Itairi Town. The mobile network would be functioning for a brief time after he had made the necessary adjustments and had convinced the strikers that it was all for the cause. He walked briskly to his little car in the car park, anonymous amidst the other rusting vehicles, then leapt out of sight into an alley as two army trucks sped along the main road a short distance away. He walked calmly to his car so as not to attract attention. He checked the boot and breathed a sigh of relief as he saw that the parcel from Miguel was still there, along with the grenade, looking like a sinister metal pineapple.

He sat in the stifling heat of the car and quietly spoke on his mobile to Miguel.

'As you see, the phones will be working for a short time. You can make your call now, Miguel.'

He listened intently as Miguel outlined his plans, then sat back and took a deep breath.

'Then we are ready. I will drive to the hotel immediately to deliver the package.'

He wondered whether to say 'God be with you' to Miguel but decided against it, and with a dramatic flourish instead whispered *'Viva La Revolucion!'*

****

Karen eventually decided it was time to come out of the bathroom. Sulking in there like a teenager wasn't very dignified and anyway, the heat in there was almost unbearable. She opened the door and, with her head held high, decided to have a sensible, adult conversation with Steve. She was surprised to see him standing out of sight by the open window, listening intently. He saw her and put his finger to his lips then jabbed it at the open window. Through the venetian blinds she could just make out someone standing on the terrace, holding a mobile to his ear. She realised it was Ian. He sounded scared out of his wits as he spoke into the phone.

'No, listen I can't talk long, I'm outside...I can't talk in my room, there's no reception, it'll have to be out here. My god, it's that bad? You mean it could happen at any time? Of course I want to help, but smuggle it...what if I'm caught?'

Karen's eyes widened in alarm. *What was going on?*

'And the package will be delivered today? But can you be sure I'll be able to get my flight...yes, yes, one o'clock tomorrow. You will wait until then before starting anything?'

There was a long pause.

'Yes, I understand. Of course, I would prefer to stay, to witness it first hand, but...yes, you're right. This is worth a hell of a lot more. Don't worry Miguel. You can count on me. OK, ok, trust me, I'll deliver it. Bye.'

Ian hung up and disappeared from view, and they heard the door of his room slam. Steve carefully shut the window of the room so as not to make any noise. He spoke to Karen in a low voice.

'What do you make of that then?'

Karen felt sick, and wished Steve hadn't started eavesdropping. 'I don't know – he said something about smuggling. You don't think...well, you don't think it's drugs do you?'

'I don't know. Before you come out he was talking about smuggling something. Then there's all that stuff about a valuable package. So what else is he going to be talking about?'

Karen's brain whirled in confusion.

'But he's a respected art critic!'

Steve scoffed. 'So...? They're all on it, aren't they? Artists. Cocaine, heroin, whatever.'

'How do you know?'

'Everybody knows. Seen it in the papers, haven't I? In their posh clubs, all sniffing cocaine off toilet seats. '

'Oh don't be so daft, you mean toilet...cisterns... don't you? Anyway, there's got to be a mistake. I'm sure it's a mistake.'

Steve grunted. 'Yeah, well, I'm keeping a close eye on that one. He wants watching.'

Karen suddenly remembered that it wasn't just Ian she was supposed to be suspicious about. 'You're just jealous,' she blurted out without thinking.

'You what?!' Steve pronounced the last letter of 'what' with such emphasis that the word sounded like 'whats'.

'Jealous of him? Come off it.'

'Alright maybe you're not jealous. Maybe I am.' She could feel the hysteria rising in her throat and forced herself to stay calm.

Steve looked genuinely upset. 'What's that supposed to mean?'

'Have you just forgotten everything that's gone on? I want to know who this Anna is.' She was quivering with restrained anger now, her fists clenched by her sides.

Steve looked helpless. 'Look, babes, just wait a bit, yeah? I can't talk about it just now. The time isn't right. Wait until tonight.'

Karen just didn't know what to think. She was sure he was up to something, but why couldn't he tell her? And what was he going to do tonight? Give her the old 'we need to talk' dumping speech? She suddenly felt the need for fresh air.

'I'm going outside to sit on the terrace. Are you coming?'

'Might as well' replied Steve. 'Nothing much going on round the pool anyway. Hardly anybody in the hotel.'

That suits me, thought Karen. She wasn't in the mood for jolly holiday activities anyway. She decided she would sit on the terrace until the afternoon heat cooled off a bit, then walk into San Itari town to see one of the churches, whether Steve liked it or not.

Outside the room she noticed that Ian was still there, but he had somehow got himself one of those packets of wine from the restaurant and was sitting dejectedly at his table, looking into middle distance and drinking a large tumbler full of the cheap fizzy drink. Pauline and Angie were on their sun loungers, engrossed in celebrity magazines.

'Hiya love, you alright?' said Pauline, looking up. Angie kept on reading.

'Yes thanks' replied Karen, putting a brave face on it, as she and Steve settled down on their loungers.

'Terrible about that man on the beach, wasn't it,' said Karen.

'Poor thing' replied Pauline. 'He was daft to pull a stunt like that, but there was no call for those revolutionaries or whatever they are to beat him up.'

Ian looked up with an angry expression. Karen suspected he was a little bit drunk.

'They weren't "revolutionaries"', he said. 'They were some sort of secret policemen.'

Pauline looked doubtful. 'Maybe they were policemen then. I've heard foreign policemen can be a bit violent sometimes. Not like ours, you know.'

Ian laughed bitterly. 'You think the British police aren't violent as well? I can tell you of hundreds of cases of police brutality in the UK, much of it against ethnic minorities.' He swigged from his tumbler of wine, sloshing a few drops over the sides and down his shirt.

Karen noticed that Steve was looking at Ian with distaste. She hoped he wasn't going to say anything about his suspicions towards Ian.

'Well then they shouldn't be coming into our country then should they?' said Angie, looking up with an expression of annoyance. 'If they don't like it, they can always go home.'

'For God's sake' breathed Ian, looking away and twiddling with his phone. There was silence but then Karen noticed that Ian was looking at her intently, and she was sure she saw his eyes flick up and down her body momentarily. He smiled.

'Oh, by the way, er Karen, I'm thinking of having a look round the church of Santa Croce in town this afternoon. There's an altarpiece by one of Goya's pupils. Perhaps you and, er, Steve would like to come? Not really my scene, but it's supposed to be a good painting.'

Steve definitely looked annoyed. He folded his arms.

'No thanks mate. We're on holiday, not at university.'

'Same thing these days' said Angie, not looking up.

Karen was adamant that she would go. 'It sounds interesting'.

'I don't think so thanks. Not under the circumstances' replied Steve.

He stressed the last word and Karen realised he was still suspicious about Ian. It was ridiculous but she felt that if she went without Steve, there would be a major row later. Despite thinking she was probably going to be dumped later, she really didn't have the energy for it. A kind of bland resignation washed over her.

'Alright, maybe some other time. But thanks for the offer.' She flashed a perfunctory smile at Ian.

Ian nodded curtly, and looked away.

Angie put her magazine down. 'I can't see the point of going round churches. Unless you're religious, like.'

'I don't know, some of them are quite interesting,' said Pauline. 'What about that one in Malta last year? That was quite interesting'.

'Oh that' snorted Angie. 'That were a right con. The guide kept going on about a miracle in this church on Malta. 'Come see the miracle, come see the miracle', he said. Well, we thought it'd be summat like a crying statue, or one of them bald kiddies what got healed, like at Lourdes. Some hope. Guess what it was?'

'An unexploded bomb' said Ian in a bored voice, taking a slurp of his wine.

Angie was stunned. 'How did you know that?'

'I've been there. It's in the Rotunda Church. Did a programme on it for BBC4 a couple of years ago. Part of a series, *Fiction and Faith*. But then I don't suppose you'd have watched that. Reactionary rubbish anyway, most of it. Actually perhaps you would have liked it in that case.'

'Oh, have you been on the telly?' asked Pauline with interest, but Ian ignored her.

Angie looked at Pauline and Ian in annoyance and resumed her anecdote.

'Anyroad, in the war, this bomb come through the roof of the church when the place was full on Sunday see, right in the middle of the aisle, rolled along and out the door, and it never went off. And they said it were a miracle!' Angie tutted with annoyance.

'Well I don't know much about religion but that sounds pretty miraculous to me,' said Pauline.

Angie was in full flow now. 'Well, what about all the other poor buggers in the war who never got a miracle? What about Coventry cathedral? If that's a miracle, you can keep it. Miracles aren't the same these days like they were in the Bible days. Little kiddies getting cured in Lourdes is right and proper, but you can't go around calling unexploded bombs miracles. That's just bad workmanship.'

Ian looked away and sighed. 'Oh well, I probably won't bother going by myself. I just thought it might be good for that course of yours. I'm not into churches one bit really. Opium of the people, and all that.'

Steve looked at Ian intently. 'Oh yeah? What does that mean, then?'

Ian looked at Steve with a bored expression. 'Religion is the opium of the people. Karl Marx.'

'That right?' Steve was looking at Ian closely.

He's definitely got it in for Ian, thought Karen. *Why bother, if he's planning on dumping me anyway?*

Ian took another swig of wine. 'I was only looking for some excuse to get out of this dump for a while. I can't go yet anyway.'

'Why's that then?' said Steve.

Ian shrugged his shoulders and looked away with a guilty expression. 'Just waiting.' He picked up his phone and began twiddling with it again. Karen thought he did look rather suspicious now.

Angie laughed. 'Well we've got plenty planned even if you haven't. We'll be on't loungers until six, then it's cocktails, then it's tea, then it's bingo and then it's karaoke, and after that there's supposed to be a hypnotist. At least there's plenty going on even if the place is grubby.'

There were a few moments of silence as Karen laid back and let the late afternoon sun warm her. The hotel did seem very quiet now – the music had stopped as had the sounds of kids playing by the pool. Despite what Angie said there didn't actually seem that much going on. She heard the sounds of heavy lorries grinding along the coast road. She looked up at the deep blue, cloudless sky and suddenly felt a long way from home.

A shadow fell over her and with professional bustle and a whiff of cheap perfume, Trisha appeared on the terrace. Everybody looked up as she flipped through the pages on her clipboard.

'Hello everybody' she trilled. 'I've just come to see that everybody is satisfied with their current present situation at this moment in time, as we speak.'

Ian gave a short bitter laugh and didn't even look up from his phone.

Steve and Pauline nodded and Karen noticed Angie at least didn't have any complaints. Something was troubling her though.

'Why's it so quiet? There doesn't seem to be anyone around.'

Karen thought she saw a look of worry cross Trisha's face but it was soon replaced by the professional smile. 'We *are* a little bit underbooked at the moment, but that's due to the situation at the airport. I'm pleased to say we are clearing the backlog due to the strike and getting a lot of the guests home.' She turned to go.

Ian looked at her with suspicion. 'If the strike's over why aren't any more people arriving here then?'

'I'm afraid that at the moment I don't have any more information in my possession at this point in time.' She turned to go.

She's definitely hiding something, thought Karen.

As she passed Ian she touched him briefly on the shoulder. 'Oh, Mr Hurst, there's a man for you in reception.'

Ian sat up suddenly in his seat. 'A man? What does he want?'

Karen noticed that Steve's eyes were flicking between Trisha and Ian with cool alertness.

'He says he has a parcel for yourself. I said I would give it to you but he's most insistent that it should be delivered to you personally in person by himself to yourself. As we don't allow non-guests in the hotel he's waiting for you in reception at this point in time.'

She gave Ian a curious look then clattered away. Ian jumped up and followed her off the terrace.

Steve stood up with a triumphant expression on his face. 'See, I told you. This is it – the drop.'

Angie looked up with a puzzled expression. 'The what?'

Karen wished he hadn't mentioned it with Pauline and Angie around. 'Steve, don't be silly...'

Steve looked around and lowered his voice. 'That bloke. He's up to something. Drugs, I reckon.'

Angie had a look of fascinated horror on her face. 'Never! Go on.'

'Surely not,' said Pauline. 'He seems decent enough, he's even been on telly.'

'Don't let that fool you' snorted Steve. 'Course he's nice – has to be to get it through customs. So as not to arouse suspicion.'

Karen felt this was all getting out of hand. With things the way they were with Steve, she wasn't in the mood to back him up unconditionally.

'I really think you shouldn't go around accusing people of things like that when you've got no proof.'

'We have got proof. We heard him talking on his mobile earlier. Said he would smuggle something out of the country that was worth a lot of money and he'd get in a lot of trouble if he got caught. What else would he be on about?'

Angie smacked a fist into her palm with a rattle of jewellery. 'I knew it. I said to meself, as soon as I saw him, I said, he's up to no good that one. Shifty.'

'Then just now he was going on about opium' continued Steve. His lip curled. 'It's disgusting. I've read about his type in the paper. They make millions, just from carrying the stuff. Moles, they call them.'

'You what?' said Angie.

'Moles. That's what they call the blokes that carry the drugs.'

Karen stifled a laugh, despite her growing unease. 'Don't you mean mules?'

Steve waved away the comment. 'Whatever. Question is, what we going to do about it?'

'Nothing,' replied Karen, emphatically. 'Because I'm sure he hasn't done anything.'

'Yeah, well you would say that,' muttered Steve.

'And what's that supposed to mean?' said Karen, her voice rising. Steve ignored her.

'Should we tell the police?' offered Pauline in a concerned voice.

Angie's lip curled.'Don't be daft. Police in these countries are in it as well. Corrupt, like. Probably helping him.'

Steve stood up. 'I'm having it out with him.'

There was a decisive note in his voice, probably the tone he'd used out in Afghanistan, thought Karen. She really hoped he wasn't going to do something stupid. She tried to make light of the situation.

'Don't be silly. You can't just go accusing people of things like that. There's proper... channels. Look, if you really think he's up to no good, let's just have a quiet word with the rep and they'll search his bags at the airport.'

Steve thought for a moment but then shook his head. 'With all the delays at the airport they probably won't bother. And what if they do search him and don't find anything? They hide this stuff in all kinds of places.'

Angie shifted uncomfortably on her lounger. 'Oh, I don't want to think about it.'

Steve was resolute. 'You got to take the law into your own hands at times like this.'

Karen saw Ian walking hurriedly towards the terrace with a large package under his arm. She suddenly realised there was going to be a nasty scene. *Some holiday this is turning out to be*, she thought.

All eyes were on Ian as he walked towards his room. Karen's heart sank as Steve blocked his path.

'Just a minute, mate.'

Ian looked up with an expression of surprise then irritation. 'Yes?'

He tried to walk round Steve but the larger man countered him. 'What's in the parcel?'

Ian swallowed. 'What's it got to do with you?'

Angie called out from her lounger. 'What you being so cagey about? He only asked a question.'

Pauline tried to shush Angie but was resolutely ignored.

Steve carried on. 'Souvenir is it? Something for the wife and kids?'

Ian tried a more conciliatory tone and gave Steve a forced smile. 'No – it's nothing to concern you, so if you'll just let me go to my room…'

'It does concern me mate. I'm making it my concern.' There was a note of icy command in Steve's voice. Upon hearing it, something seemed to snap in Ian. The critic tried to push Steve out of the way. He might as well have tried to push a statue.

Ian's voice had risen to a strained pitch and Karen watched in growing horror as his face grew bright red.

'Who the bloody hell do you think you are? Get out of my way, you…yob!'

'Right. That's it,' snapped Steve, and grabbed the parcel deftly from under Ian's arm.

'Don't touch that you idiot!' screamed Ian. 'You've no idea how much that's worth!'

Angie stood up and strode over as Steve began to rip the wrapping paper from the parcel. She looked Ian up and down with disdain.

'Worth a lot of money eh? Looks like we were right. Disgusting. Your sort make me sick.'

Karen felt this had all got way out of hand and was desperate to calm things down. She tried to stand between Steve and Ian. 'Steve, stop it, Mr Hurst, I mean Ian, I'm sorry, it's all a mistake…'

Steve finally tore off the last of the wrapping paper and looked at the contents of the parcel. His eyebrows shot up in surprise and puzzlement.

'What the hell is *this*?'

Eleven

In the sultry heat of the late afternoon sun, Del Toro's men began their long awaited clean up of the island's revolutionaries. In several key points in San Itairi town and in various villages across the island, trucks screeched to a halt and black clad soldiers jumped out. These were not the callow conscripts or elderly reservists guarding the beaches, but the crack troops of the *Guardia Presidencial,* eager for violent action like unleashed fighting dogs. Doors were kicked down and men dragged from their homes and bundled into vehicles as the sound of sporadic gunfire rattled in the air, and the acrid smell of smoke bombs drifted across the narrow cobbled streets.

****

Chaos had broken out in Miguel Corantes' cave headquarters in the northern part of the island. Men ran back and forth and piled weapons and ammunition into decrepit pickup trucks outside which sped off in clouds of blue exhaust fumes, bumping along the rutted back roads to pre-planned meeting points. Amidst it all Miguel barked orders and hastily scribbled notes for his motorcycle messengers. He looked up in surprise as a figure rushed into the cave, his clothes dishevelled and his body soaked in sweat. It was Jose.

The two men embraced. Miguel held his shoulders in a rigid grip to calm him and looked deep into his eyes.

'Did you give the parcel to the Englishman?'

Jose could barely catch his breath, and began to gabble. *'Si, si*, I gave it, as you asked.'

Miguel sighed in relief. 'You have done well. It is too late for it to be taken from the country, but the government will not risk harming an Englishman because of it.'

Jose chattered on excitedly. 'But the soldiers nearly caught me. Miguel, the island has gone mad, the government men are killing anyone they think is with us, we...'

Miguel cut him off by gripping his shoulders even more strongly and piercing him with an authoritative glare.

'I know Jose. It has begun. Freedom is almost within our grasp. Now, go, go, take a rifle and go to your meeting place.'

As Jose nodded and scurried away, Miguel picked up his sub-machine gun and prepared to leave with the last of his men. He called out to his men.

'Viva el liberacion! Viva San Itairi!'

A huge cheer echoed and re-echoed from the walls of the cave.

****

Ian trembled with suppressed fury as he watched Steve wave the contents of the parcel around to the assembled group on the terrace, who huddled round in fascination.

That's all I need, he thought. *This shaven headed moron is going to ruin it.*

Steve continued to look at the object with puzzlement. 'What is it? This isn't drugs.'

This time Ian was puzzled. *What on earth is this twat on about?* he thought.

'Drugs? What are you talking about? For God's sake don't wave it around!'

Steve held up the object. 'It's just a bit of canvas, with some paint on.'

Angie bustled round them like an angry wasp, alternatively poking Ian in the chest and looking round to the group.

'What you got that for? What's he want that for?'

Karen stepped forwards and smiled weakly at Ian.

'I'm sorry…we thought….we overheard you on the phone talking about smuggling something and Steve thought…'

Suddenly Ian saw everything clearly and his mouth dropped open in disbelief. It was like the paedophile thing all over again. *My god, how deluded could these people be?*

He laughed out loud. 'You heard me on the phone and thought it was – drugs! Oh my...oh my God, that's priceless!'

Angie's face was in full bulldog mode. 'Well I'm glad you see the funny side of it. I don't.'

Steve looked a little sheepish and stepped back from Ian. 'Listen mate, no offence, I...'

Ian carried on laughing, pushing back his hair with both hands and looking round at nobody in particular. He suddenly visualised how fantastic the whole thing would sound in one expertly crafted Twitter posting, if only his phone would work.

'Oh God that's brilliant. Wait 'til I tell them at the Groucho. My God, you people...talk about Middle England...it's beyond a joke.'

Steve's sheepish expression turned to embarrassment. 'Look, it's just we thought...well to be honest, we thought you was up to no good. Here, look, you can have this back.'

He proffered the canvas to Ian who grabbed it and wiped imaginary dust from it with his sleeve.

Angie still eyed Ian suspiciously and nudged Pauline. 'I still don't trust him. What if there's drugs hidden in the frame of that thing?'

'Oh for God's sake Angie don't be silly,' said Pauline. 'It's just a picture frame.'

Karen looked relieved but fascinated. 'Yes…what is it, Ian? Is it a painting?' She craned forward to look at the canvas with its alternating stripes of colour.

Angie tutted. 'Don't be daft. That's not a painting.'

Ian's outburst of hilarity had died down a little and he turned to face the group, a slight smile of pride on his face.

'I don't know why I'm bothering to tell you, but it's one of the most valuable works of art of this decade, in both financial and political terms.'

Steve looked at the canvas closely. 'What? How much is it worth, then?'

Ian propped the canvas on a plastic chair and straightened it. He guessed that it was safe; nobody in a place like this was likely to have any idea of its significance.

'Not that it's any of your business, but in order to stop you buggering about with it any further, I should warn you that it was last valued, somewhat conservatively, at four million pounds.'

He folded his arms and waited for a response.

Steve whistled. 'Je-sus.'

Angie laughed. 'Four million quid, for that? Don't be daft.'

'I think I've seen it,' Karen exclaimed excitedly. 'In your art book. Isn't it by Corantes?'

Ian smiled. 'Well spotted.' *At least there's hope for her*, thought Ian. *Shame she's with that oaf.*

Pauline looked interested as well. 'By who?'

Ian folded his arms. 'By none other than Miguel Corantes. The artist I've just interviewed actually.'

Angie now looked a little confused and her voice had a note of disbelief. 'But how can that be worth four million pound? It looks like a five year old done it.'

Pauline laughed. 'Well, it's, it's modern art, isn't it? They have all sorts like that these days. Beds and things in galleries, and sharks in tanks. I've seen it in the paper.'

Ian wondered just what sort of rubbish she'd read about. He felt a sudden need to reach out to these people, to try to get them to understand something of life outside their narrow minded prejudices.

Angie went on, waving a cigarette around and stabbing the air with it to illustrate the points of her argument.

'Well I don't believe it. I think he's having us on. I've had enough of this feller. Thinks he can have a laugh at us 'cos we're just normal people.'

The combination of wine, heat and stress finally caused Ian's temper to snap. He stood up much faster than he should have done, causing his head to spin a little and his chair to lurch dangerously backwards.

'Normal! What would you know about normal? Listen, *love,* I'M normal!' He felt a guilty thrill at the use of the word 'love'. He hoped they realised he was using it ironically.

The assembled group were staring at him as he continued. He felt an oratorical power sweeping through him, urging him to get them to see things as they really were.

'People like *me* are normal. People who travel, who are cosmopolitan, instead of narrow minded nationalists, who want to be with ordinary people of all different cultures. People who read books and listen to Radio Four and believe in social justice. *That's* normal. You're some bloody throwback even the *Daily Mail* would think was bigoted. Christ, the stuff you lot come out with!'

Ian waved his arms around, looking at the shabby loungers and the union jack towel fluttering from a balcony in the distance.

'This place! It's like Blackpool, only less cultured! You've no interest in anything, you people, have you? Nothing exists outside your own little world. There's a whole country of real people out there – real, working, struggling people, fighting against an authoritarian government, and you just sit there with your blue drinks and your bingo and your union jack shorts and your tabloids and you couldn't give a toss about anything else!'

He sat down, exhausted. The group were too stunned to say anything, but Steve stepped forward.

'You British, mate?'

Ian looked up in confusion. He felt decidedly odd after his outburst.

'I *said*, Are. You. British?'

Oh yes, thought Ian. *I get it.* I'm not 'British' enough for these people. *Well good.* Patriotism, next to religion, he thought, was the cause of pretty much every problem in history. If they wanted to debate *that*, he was up for the challenge.

'I don't recognise national boundaries actually, but 'British' is what it says on my passport if you must know. What about it?'

The women looked on with rapt attention. Angie was puffing furiously on her cigarette, her head turning from Steve to Ian like a spectator at a tennis match. This time it was Steve's turn, but rather than ranting, he spoke coolly and firmly, looking at Ian with disdain.

'You act like you care more about the people here than your own lot. Some of us like *all this* as you call it. We're here on holiday. We want to relax, have a few drinks, have a few laughs. We don't go abroad to save the world, like bloody Bono. You bang on about ordinary working people – what do you think we all are? There's blokes here working their arses off back home to afford a couple of weeks' holiday with the family. Blokes doing work you couldn't dream about. There's a man in that bar from Essex who works 12 hours a day cleaning out drains, probably on the minimum wage. He says saved up for two years to come here to give his wife a treat for their wedding anniversary. Ever done that? That's struggling people mate – in your own bloody country under your own nose, and just because they're not wearing sombreros and singing the red flag you think they're scum.'

There was a pause. Ian looked slightly sheepish but was determined that he wouldn't be topped in argument by the likes of Steve.

'Rubbish. I have complete respect for all working people.' He crossed his arms in triumph.

Steve smiled. 'Alright then. How many working class people – British ones – do you actually know?'

Ian swallowed. He suddenly felt very awkward. This kind of debate was all very well online, at dinner parties or with a carefully vetted Radio Four discussion panel, but under the burning sun and hostile gazes of a group of package tourists, it was another matter.

'Well, I...there's the cleaning lady...and...well, actually she's Polish...'

Steve laughed and the others joined in, although Ian noticed Karen was looking at him with something approaching pity.

Ian determined to regain the moral high ground. *What is he on about, the working class*? As if it was still the nineteen-fifties.

'This is completely irrelevant. There's no such thing as class now anyway. British people have undreamed of luxury compared to most people in the world. There are immigrant workers in our own country who...'

Steve cut him off. 'I'm not talking about them though am I? Nobody made them come over. I don't grudge them trying to make a living same as anyone else. *I'm* talking about ordinary, British, working class doing their best to get by, who've paid tax and insurance all their lives.'

He looked at Ian with thinly disguised contempt.

'You and all your lot who run the country, with your big papers and your dinner parties, you say you care about ordinary people but you don't know any and you don't want to know any 'cos they aren't into the same things you are, and that's why you can't stand places like this.'

There was silence as the two men stared each other down. Pauline cleared her throat but before she could say anything, Angie bought her fist down on the plastic table with a thump and rattle of jewellery.

'Well I'm not working class. Every house in our street has a conservatory, and off street parking. Just because I'm not from London, and don't talk all posh, or know about art, it doesn't mean I'm scum, you know.'

Karen finally spoke, putting her hand on Steve's shoulder. 'Look, let's all calm down, eh? I'm sure you didn't mean all that, did you Ian, Steve? We've all just got a bit hot and bothered.'

Ian was now feeling very unsettled. He hadn't exactly been beaten in an argument, but he felt he'd come out of it rather badly. He'd never thought of himself before as the sort of person who ran the country; he was anti-establishment and had always fought against the ruling class. But this man thought he was a part of all that.

Ian ran his hands through his hair. 'Well, perhaps I was a bit....'

'Least said, soonest mended,' chipped in Pauline, brightly.

'Huh' said Angie with disdain. 'Anyway, I might not know much, but I know *that's* not art.' She pointed to the canvas on the chair. 'Art's things like the, the...*Mona Lisa*. Now if he'd nicked *that* I'd be impressed.

Ian bridled. 'I haven't "nicked" anything. I've been given it to look after and take back to London.'

'Why?' asked Steve.

'Perhaps if you'd watched anything on the television other than football, or gone any further than the hotel bar, you might have realised the political situation here is somewhat precarious, to say the least.'

'Don't be daft, it'll all blow over,' said Angie.

Ian frowned. 'Well the owner of this painting didn't seem to think so. He was willing to risk four million pounds for the sake of art.'

Angie laughed. 'Well I wouldn't have risked four pence on it.'

Karen looked at the painting again. 'What's it called?'

Ian smiled proudly. '*Deliverance*'.

Steve looked puzzled. 'Wasn't that a film with Burt Reynolds?'

'It doesn't look much like Burt Reynolds,' said Pauline.

'It doesn't look much like anything at all,' replied Steve.

Ian smiled again. 'Actually that's where you're wrong. Unlike most of Corantes' works, this one is entirely figurative.' He picked up the canvas with loving care and holding it up to the light to admire it. It really was breathtaking, he thought.

'Entirely what?' said Pauline.

'He means it's meant to look like something. I think,' said Karen.

Angie pursed her lips and peered at the painting. 'I should hope so too, or what's the point of a painting? But that don't look like anything.'

'Again, if you knew anything about the country you were in, you might recognise it,' replied Ian.

Karen's face suddenly lit up. 'Oh hang on, I know what it is – it was in my guidebook. It's a flag, isn't it?'

Ian smiled. At least somebody here had half a brain cell, he thought. 'Well done.'

'What kind of flag?' asked Steve.

'It's a painting of the flag of the People's Democratic Party of San Itairi,' said Ian. 'It's been banned by the right wing government here since the coup, years ago. That's why Corantes doesn't want it to stay on the island while the government forces are rampaging around. If the authorities find it, it'll be destroyed and he'll be arrested as a subversive. He could get thrown into jail for this and tortured. So could I, if they knew I had it.'

'But it's just a flag,' said Pauline. 'It's not even that when you think about it. It's just a painting of a flag.'

Ian fixed Pauline and the rest of the group with a gaze that was almost messianic.

'It's more than that – it's a symbol of defiance that's an embarrassment to the fascists as long as they're in power, and they'll stop at nothing to get hold of it. You realise I could be killed if I'm found with this?'

'Oh my God it's *worse* than drugs,' wailed Angie. 'Why couldn't you just have had drugs instead?'

Ian gave her a withering look and began to wrap up the painting.

'Now that you've uncovered my little secret perhaps I could ask you all to keep it quiet?'

'Of course, we won't tell anyone.' Karen smiled and looked relieved.

Steve turned away and stretched out on his lounger. 'I don't want to know anything more about it. Let's just forget it.'

Ian began to feel some dignity and control returning. The thought of his flight back to civilisation revitalised him. He went into his room and began to pack his things.

****

Trisha was in her room, getting ready for what she euphemistically thought to herself as her 'charm offensive' on Ian. She'd got her best underwear on, a posh black set from Marks and Spencer with a push up bra that showed off her ample bust to great advantage. She decided she'd keep that on whatever happened. She could hold her stomach in indefinitely, but there was no way she could defy gravity. Black hold up stockings completed the look. She doused herself in her best perfume, *Red Sin* by Christina Aguilera, that she'd got cheap at the Duty Free because the bottle was cracked. She then slipped on her turquoise rep's uniform and checked in the mirror for VPL. *Not bad*, she thought, admiring herself in the mirror and putting on a last touch of lipgloss. *Now let's see what Mr James Bond Hotel Inspector has to put in his report about this.*

Suddenly there was a loud banging on the flimsy door of her room and a man burst in before Trisha could even reply.

It was Fuego, the receptionist. His normally smart uniform was dishevelled and he was out of breath.

'Trisha, Trisha, at last I found you, come quickly, quickly!'

For a moment Trisha wondered if this was some sort of come on. She'd always had a bit of a soft spot for Fuego but he'd never seemed interested in her for some reason.

Trisha sighed. 'What's the problem Fuego?' She guessed it would be something routine and tedious. Probably that bulldog-faced woman complaining again.

Fuego gasped to catch his breath. 'Manager say…manager say all staff have to come to office now. Is big big problem!'

Trisha groaned. 'Someone hasn't done their business in the pool again have they?'

Fuego looked confused and turned to go. 'Business? No, no is not about business. Is very bad – big, big fighting on island and British Embassy tell manager everyone must go. Is revelation!'

Trisha was completely confused now but began to follow Fuego out of the door. He did look really worried. What did 'revelation' mean, she wondered. *Didn't they make suitcases?* The manager was hopeless at the best of times.

'It's what, Fuego?'

Fuego managed to compose himself. 'Sorry, I mean, is...*revolution*!'

****

On the terrace outside her room, Pauline was enjoying the last of the sun but she couldn't concentrate on her celebrity magazine. The hotel seemed eerily deserted and in the distance beyond the terrace she had seen a couple of reps almost running to the reception area. She'd also had a quick look over the wall to the beach and noticed a lot of the soldiers running about carrying equipment. This really wasn't the relaxing holiday she'd been hoping for.

And that argument between the two men earlier. What were they like? At least they'd gone into their rooms now so there'd be a bit of peace and quiet before tea. She didn't like unpleasantness of any sort, but she hated seeing people arguing on holiday. She noticed it had put Angie's back up as well. All that talk of drugs had rattled her and she was smoking one cigarette after another.

Angie drummed her fingers on her lounger and looked intently at Pauline. 'To think this place is meant to be all exclusive. The rubbish they let in! Smuggling paintings and talking to us like we're dirt.'

Pauline looked around anxiously. 'I think it's best if we don't mention that painting anymore. After all he did say he could get in trouble with it.'

'Don't be daft! I'm complaining to the staff about this. I'm not having people going round with illegal paintings and talking about socialism. This is a family resort. Now where's that rep?'

Pauline's nerves were rattled. She had a nasty feeling something was going very wrong on this holiday. What if those reps running about had something to do with the smuggled painting? Maybe even the soldiers on the beach had found out about it.

'Oh for heaven's sake Angie will you just leave it alone?'

Angie's eyes flashed fury. 'Leave it alone! That's your whole life isn't it? Turn a blind eye, don't cause a fuss, least said, soonest mended!'

'I just think…'

'I honestly don't know why I bother inviting you on holiday with me. You never enjoy yourself. You just sit there.'

Pauline was starting to have enough of all this. She was a patient woman, but this was getting a bit much.

'Well as a matter of fact…'

Angie cut her off. 'Oh never mind. Here comes the rep. I'm going to tell her about this smuggling business.'

Pauline saw Trisha rushing, as fast as she could in her high heels, up to their terrace. Had she already found out about the smuggling? Pauline hoped not. There'd been enough excitement on this holiday already and the last thing they wanted was to have to go to some foreign police station to make a statement.

Trisha grabbed for support on a plastic table, her jiggling bust coming to a halt a split second after the rest of her. She carried a clipboard and used it to fan her face as she gasped her breath. Pauline noticed several other reps and residents rushing with cases towards reception. What on earth was going on?

'Are you alright, love?' she said with concern.

Trisha plonked down her clipboard and continued the ineffectual fanning of her face, in the way that Pauline had noticed girls did when they won those singing competitions on the telly.

Trisha called out to nobody in particular. 'Ladies and gentleman, if you could all remain calm. Remain calm!'

She took a large swig of Ian's wine which had been left on the table. Alerted by the shouting, Steve and Karen came out of their rooms, soon followed by Ian.

Steve looked grumpy. Pauline wondered if he'd had another row with his girlfriend. They didn't seem to be getting on that well, she thought.

'We are calm,' said Pauline. 'What are you so worked up about?'

Angie stepped forward. 'Look love, I've got a complaint…'

Trisha ignored her and continued trying to catch her breath.

'If...if I could just have your attention now at this point in time, I'm afraid we do have a little bit of a situation on our hands.'

'What do you mean?' asked Angie, angrily.

'I'm afraid that at this time we have a little bit of an emergency situation on our hands…I'm sorry to say that I have been asked by the British Embassy to ask all British citizens, or citizens of...' She checked an official paper with some hurried scrawls of writing on it.

'Of Her Majesty's other realms and territories… who at this time are in the hotel, to prepare to leave.'

'What the hell's going on?' said Ian. 'Not that I care really, since I'm leaving anyway.'

Angie folded her arms. Pauline knew that look in her eyes, she wasn't having any of it. *She'd have stayed on the Titanic just to get her money's worth*, thought Pauline.

'Leave? You must be joking, we've only just got here. We've got aquarobics in half an hour.'

Karen looked concerned and touched Trisha on the shoulder. 'Look, what's going on, are you sure you're ok?'

Trisha took a deep breath and straightened herself up. She had a glazed look in her eyes.

'I regret to announce that at this time there has been a political coup here in San Itairi. I can assure you there is no need for panic!'

She turned and took another swig of wine from the table. Pauline wasn't quite sure what a coup was – was it some sort of election? It didn't sound too good anyway.

Angie was still nonplussed. 'Well what's that got to do with us? We're not into politics here. We're just on holiday.'

Trisha riffled violently through the papers on her clipboard until she found one that prompted her. She read most of it out loud.

'I'm sorry to say that at this time, to the best of our knowledge, the lawful government of San Itairi has been overthrown by an armed uprising and a number of people, including some British tourists, have been caught in the crossfire and regretfully killed. The rebel forces are pursuing the remainder of the army across the island and we are of the opinion that a limited amount of military combat may be taking place here in the near future. Therefore we, and the British Embassy, would advise, that the hotel is evacuated, in the interests of health and safety.'

There was a sound of shouted orders in Spanish outside the compound wall, and the roar of diesel engines as a column of lorries sped past. Pauline swallowed down panic as she heard glass breaking somewhere near reception and a child begin howling. Angie's face went white and she gripped the side of her lounger for support.

'Oh my God! They're going to kill us….they're going to kill us!'

Suddenly Pauline felt a shift in her authority. Up until now she'd followed what Angie had said. But this called for a cool head. She didn't even think about it, she just felt calm and in control. She shook Angie firmly by the shoulders.

'Now come on, don't be silly. Let's get our bags packed. Come on Ange, pull yourself together. Nobody's going to get killed.'

Up until now Ian had been listening open mouthed but now he strode up to Trisha and grabbed her arm.

'Look, I need to know everything about this. I'll need to contact my editor. We've got to get this out to the media.'

He shook her arm and Trisha looked at him blankly. Pauline could see she was on the edge of losing control. Fortunately Steve stepped in. She remembered he'd been been in the army in Iraq or Afghanistan or something. That probably explained why he was calm. She decided it would be best for her and Angie if they stuck near him.

Steve spoke to Ian firmly. 'Look, you, let her do her job. You can talk to her later.'

He firmly manoeuvred Ian out of the way, who drew back, sulkily.

'Where are they taking us? Where do we have to go?' said Steve, putting his arm round Trisha and looking down at her clipboard. She seemed to brighten a bit and looked at her papers again.

'I have been advised that we will be staying in the British Embassy compound until further notice. The coach will be leaving from reception in 15 minutes.'

Hearing his, Angie seemed to calm down a little. 'Oh…British Embassy you say? Do they have a pool there, d'ye think…?'

Steve laughed. 'I doubt it. We went past it on the way in from the airport. It's only a little place. God knows how we'll all fit in there. Still, could be worse I suppose.'

Pauline tried to ease the situation with a joke. She vaguely remembered a school history lesson about something like this happening abroad.

'Let's hope it don't turn out to be like the Black Hole of Calcutta!'

Angie looked confused. 'Don't be daft. Calcutta's in India. This is Central America.'

The hotel had gone eerily calm; all they could hear now was the sound of the waves breaking on the shore below the compound wall. Steve drew in his breath sharply and looked around at the group.

'A right load of crap this holiday's turned out to be. Come on everyone, we'd better get packed.'

Twelve

An hour later, Karen paced nervously around the hotel's front drive as Steve sat sullenly in reception. Angie and Pauline were sitting on their huge cases in the lobby, chain smoking, while Ian paced up and down trying to get a signal on his mobile and swearing under his breath. There didn't seem to be anyone else left in the hotel.

There hadn't been enough room on the coaches for everyone. Oddly enough, everybody seemed to be staying calm, but Steve had tried to force the driver to take Karen and had nearly come to blows with an Embassy official supervising the evacuation. In the end she'd stepped off and told Steve she was staying with him. To be honest, she wondered if she should have bothered. She still hadn't got to the bottom of this business with that other woman and she wondered if she ever would now.

She sighed and took a last look at the drive. They'd said another coach would be along in twenty minutes but that had been half an hour ago. Her feet crunched on the sticky remains of a tray of drinks that had got knocked over as the holidaymakers rushed to escape.

Steve stood up as she came towards him. He looked at his watch.

'What's happened to that rep? The coach was supposed to be picking us up ten minutes ago.'

'Perhaps we'd better have a look round the hotel again, shall I go this time?'

Pauline stood up and walked over to them, quickly looking at Angie. 'Oh I'll go love, I'm that nervous I need to do something or I'll go mental.'

Steve sat down again. 'I wouldn't bother. The first time I went to that office the bloke said he didn't know what was happening and the second time there was nobody there.'

Angie stubbed out her cigarette and checked the packet clutched in her hand, screwing it up when she found it to be empty.

'This is disgusting. That last load of people got on their coach at least an hour ago. Them Germans were on the bus quicker than you could say "Dunkirk". We must be about the only people left in the place now.'

Steve laughed grimly. 'Yeah, I see most of the staff made sure they were on the first coach out. Whatever happened to the captain going down with his ship?'

Angie looked alarmed again. 'What was that – did you say they're putting us on a ship?'

'No, I mean all the entertainers and that, they buggered off quick smart.' He sucked his teeth in disgust and rattled the small change in his shorts pockets.

'Oh, yeah – I had a word with that bloke who plays the keyboard in the bar. He was taking up two seats on one of the coaches with his synthetizer or whatever you call it. I said shouldn't you be staying behind to keep up morale with a few songs, like on the Titanic? He told me to piss off. I said good riddance, you were no Richard Clayderman anyway.'

Karen stifled a laugh. She wondered if that woman ever stopped complaining. It was nerves, she supposed. She would have liked to have snuggled up close to Steve but her feelings were in a whirl of confusion.

Pauline jumped up. 'Shush, shush, I think I can hear an engine!'

Over the sound of cicadas beginning their dusk chorus, they could hear a straining engine somewhere beyond the end of the driveway.

Ian rushed to the door, a look of wild relief on his face. 'Thank God for that. It must be the coach.'

'Quiet, quiet, everybody stop talking'. Steve waved his arms for quiet then cocked his head to one side.

'That doesn't sound like a coach...'

He strode to the door and peered down the driveway, narrowing his eyes against the orange rays of the setting sun. Suddenly he jumped back into the lobby.

'Christ, it's a tank! There's three or four tanks, about half a mile up the road, coming this way!'

Karen felt a sickening lurch in her bowels and for a moment thought she was going to be sick – or worse – but in seconds the feeling was gone. Instinctively she ran to Steve and grabbed him.

There was an ear-splitting roar and momentarily the lobby went dark. Karen looked out of the door to see a jet fighter pass impossibly low over the hotel; surely, she thought, it must have hit the roof? Seconds later however it reappeared over the pool area, its cannons rattling, and then was gone. Karen felt her ears pop and a huge shudder shake the hotel, followed by an enormous crash as some sort of bomb or rocket hit the accommodation block on the far side of the pool. She fell to the floor and was momentarily deafened, her ears ringing as they did sometimes if she'd been in a loud club. Dust and debris billowed into the lobby.

Karen felt Steve pick her up and she saw Angie gnawing on her fists and moaning, rocking herself back and forth on the floor as she gazed in horror through the hotel doors.

Pauline grabbed her and pulled her to her feet, shaking her. 'Angie, Angie, come on, snap out of it'.

Karen wondered for a minute if Pauline would slap her, like they did in films, but Angie obediently got up and primly dusted herself down, then clung to Pauline for support.

Steve ushered everyone together and began leading the way out of the lobby. He had a note of command in his voice that Karen had never heard before, even when he was angry.

'Everybody, come on, get up, get out of here, through into the compound. Quick.'

They raced out of the lobby into what she supposed was the dubious security of the walled hotel compound, but the sight of the ruined apartment block on the far side didn't do much to calm her. Ian was rushing around wildly, taking pictures of everything with his iphone, thrusting it in every direction like the plunger of a demented Dalek.

Steve shepherded the small group over to the wall away from the direction in which the tanks were approaching.

'Everybody get down, get as close to the wall as you can and keep your hands over your heads. Keep out of the open. Get under these tables.' He began pulling the plastic bar tables over to the wall and Karen crawled under one. She felt a reassuring pat from Steve's hand on her shoulder as she did so. The rattle of automatic gunfire grew louder and Karen heard strange whining, pinging noises which she supposed must be ricochets. She wondered what protection a plastic table would offer against a bullet.

The group did as he ordered, curling up against the thick whitewashed wall. Steve crouched low and from time to time looked quickly over the wall then ducked back down. Ian was still rushing around, sticking his phone over the wall and snapping away.

Steve shouted to him. 'You too – or do you want to get your head blown off?'

Ian ignored him and continued to run around. 'Stop ordering us about. We need to tell them to stop shooting – it's nothing to do with us – we're British, I'm a pacifist for God's sake!'

Steve shrugged his shoulders. 'Everybody keep down. I think we'll be ok. There's another lot on the other side of the hotel that they're shooting at, not us.'

Ian was in a frenzy, ducking and diving around the pool area and snapping away at anything that moved, his hair covered in dust and his glasses askew. His voice had risen to an alarmingly high pitch. 'What the hell do you know about it?'

'I was in the army for four years mate, so I might know a bit more about being shot at than you.'

Ian nodded his head wildly. 'Oh, the army,' he said, sarcastically. 'That doesn't surprise me one bit. I bet you wish you've got a gun now. Well now perhaps you'll know what it's like now to be an innocent civilian on the receiving end for a change.'

Karen felt fury rising up in her. She could gladly have throttled Ian.

Steve chuckled. 'I'm not too worried. I saw scarier kids in Kabul than that lot out there – proper rabble, not even got uniforms. Some of them haven't even got guns. Keep down and we'll be ok.'

Ian stood up, ducking his head as shots cracked past. He had a look of triumph on his face.

'Then that means they're the worker's party – not the government troops. Why the hell are they firing at us? We're on their side!'

Steve glared at him. 'We're not on anyone's side mate – we're stuck in crossfire between that lot and the lot over there and I'd advise you to keep your head down if you want to keep it on your shoulders.'

Angie tried to squeeze closer to the wall and began a strange wailing as Pauline tried to comfort her.

'Oh God I don't want to die!' She clenched her eyes shut and began muttering. 'Hail Mary, who art in heaven,…oh I can't remember the rest!'

'Look we're not going to die' snapped Karen, then tried to speak more comfortingly. 'Come on, they're surely not going to kill innocent people, you know, civilians, are they? What if they just don't know we're here and think the place is empty?'

Steve bit his lip. 'Babes, you could be right – there was nobody at that desk and we haven't seen anyone official around at all.'

Through the intermittent gunfire, Karen thought she heard someone calling from reception. It was hard to make out anything in the evening gloom, but then she realised it was Trisha. She was making her way around the pool in a ducking and weaving motion, her clipboard held over her head for protection as stray bullets whined above.

'Ladies and gentlemen, ladies and gentlemen…can I ask for a moment of your time at this time?'

Pauline spoke up with her new found authority. 'What the hell's going on – we thought you'd left us! Where's that coach?'

Trisha reached the relative safety of the wall and crouched down, smoothing her skirt in a prim movement despite the soot and grime that covered her face, hair, and clothes. She seemed to have regained some of her former brightness.

'I regret to inform you that due to the current military action, the coach has been suspended.'

Karen gaped. 'What do you mean?'

'I mean that due to the current military action, the coach has been suspended. Over a cliff.'

'Oh my God, was anybody hurt?' said Karen, although she felt a wave of guilty relief that they hadn't manage to catch the coach after all.

Trisha smiled 'I am pleased to inform you that everybody escaped unhurt, although Stefano the driver had his leg crushed under the coach.'

'Oh the poor love, will he be alright?' said Pauline.

'Fortunately it was his artificial leg that was crushed,' said Trisha. 'It should be alright after a bit of spot welding.'

This whole situation has become totally unreal, thought Karen, vaguely wondering if she was dreaming it all.

'So what's happening?' she asked.

Trisha looked at her clipboard, then looked up as she noticed it held nothing but torn fragments of paper. 'The other guests have been escorted to the British Embassy on foot by Stefano. At this time I have come back to escort all remaining guests, that is to say, you.'

There was a ragged cheer from the group which was cut short by another rattle of automatic gunfire outside the compound.

Ian tried to stand up then ducked down again as more shots rang out, a furious expression on his face.

'Look, how the hell can we go anywhere? We've got to get them to stop shooting at us. Tell them we're, I mean, I'm press – journalism – I used to work for the BBC, for God's sake, I'm neutral!'

Pauline had crawled on her hands and knees a little way along the wall, and now turned back.

'There's soldiers shooting outside the front door. We can't get out that way.'

Karen had a flash of inspiration and pointed to the other side of the pool. 'What about over that wall?'

Steve shook his head. 'No good – that goes straight over the cliff edge. It must be fifty feet onto the rocks.'

Pauline looked back through the reception doors again and shouted. 'Oh no, those tanks are coming right towards us!'

The clanking and rattling of the tanks on the drive could be heard clearly now, as they made their slow, inexorable way up the hotel drive.

Angie scowled. 'Just think of the mess they've made of that lovely lawn.'

Steve bobbed his head over the wall momentarily again.

'It's not us they want,' he said. 'It's those soldiers over there shooting over our heads. They must think they're being shot at from in here or something. So we've got to make sure they know we're not part of that lot. We've got to let them know we're here somehow.'

Angie looked around wide-eyed. 'Well somebody's got to go and tell them, it's your responsibility, you go!' She made shoo-ing gestures to Trisha.

Pauline tutted angrily. 'Don't be daft, she could get her head blown off. Let me think for a minute. We need to paint a sign, saying, er, saying, 'British, don't shoot'.

Karen's eyes widened in mounting panic. 'There isn't time. They're nearly up the drive now. And what if they can't read English?'

Steve clapped his hands together. 'A white flag, we need a white flag. Quick, get something white.'

Ian laughed wildly. 'For God's sake that only happens in films!'

'You got any better suggestions?' yelled Steve, as a rattle of gunfire exploded over the compound. 'I've seen it in the army – in Afghan villages, people waving white things out of windows – tablecloths, anything, just so they don't get shot at.'

'But there aren't any tablecloths here' said Pauline.

Angie nodded. 'That's right. I always thought this place was a bit common.'

Steve was looking desperately around the pool area. 'Well sheets then – bed sheets, or, or towels.'

Karen almost jumped up to run to her room, but checked herself despairingly. 'But the sheets and towels here are all navy blue, aren't they?'

'And you know why that is,' said Angie. 'So's they don't show the dirt. Told you they don't clean proper in these places.' Angie was talking to herself now. She seemed to have lost all grip on reality.

Ian shouted. 'Look this is ridiculous. They've stopped now anyway. I'm going to have to reason with them. They won't shoot when they know who I am'.

He fumbled in his bag and brought out a card which said 'National Union of Journalists: Press' which he flourished to the group in triumph.

Steve squatted forward and pushed Ian out of the way. He raced along the wall and looked through the reception doors, then hurried back. This time when he spoke, it was in a whisper.

'They've stopped alright. But that's because they're reloading. They're taking shells out of the spare stock. Seem to be making a balls-up of it and all, like they've never done it before.'

Ian hissed. 'Because they haven't you idiot. They're not soldiers, can't you grasp that? They're ordinary people like you and me, that's why we've got to talk to them, not piss about with white flags like bloody boy scouts!'

Steve spoke through gritted teeth. 'I'm telling you, if you go out there you're dead. If they aren't trained proper they won't act rational under fire. They think they're being shot at from in here and they won't stop for tea and a chat, they'll blast their way in and wipe out anyone they see.'

As if to illustrate the point, more shots whizzed overhead and the tank engines revved angrily. They could hear shouted orders and hatches slamming shut. Time seemed to have lost all meaning. Karen felt like they had been crouching by this wall for days, yet it had only been a few minutes.

Suddenly Trisha pointed to a white block of flats beyond the hotel, which was lit up gold in the setting sun.

'Look, somebody's waving a flag over that building, and those other tanks are just driving past it. It's not a white flag though...'

Karen looked and screeched with joy, then lowered her voice. 'Oh my God, It's that flag, that flag like the painting!'

Steve looked. 'You're right.' He turned to Ian. 'Didn't you say that was, that was their symbol or something, their revolution flag?'

Ian looked on with fascination, taking a shot of the scene with his iphone.

'Yes, you're right, they must be raising them to show solidarity, look, there's another going up.'

He pointed to another half-finished white apartment block on the hills close to the hotel. 'There's two more over there, and the tanks are moving away from those buildings.'

Pauline's voice was shaky with panic. Angie had gone scarily quiet and she drew her closer to her.

'That's because they're all coming over here! If only we had one of those flags…'

Steve snapped his fingers. 'I've got an idea. Quick, where's that painting?'

In an instant, he lunged at Ian's case and ripped open the catches, tossing clothing aside as he easily found the large canvas. He began to tear off the wrapping.

Ian howled in horror as he saw what Steve was about to do. His voice rose to a high pitch.

'What the hell are you…Oh no. Oh no you don't *mate*. Not with that!'

Again Karen felt her ears pop and the ground shake, then a huge roar as several shells tore into the reception area. Despite the ringing in her ears she could hear staccato gunfire from beyond it, coming over the wall. Through a pall of smoke she could see that only a heap of rubble now remained where the reception building had been. She could see all the way down the drive now, and saw the first of the tanks nosing its way through the debris into the hotel compound like Steve had said they would. She realised now she was praying under her breath, over and over, *please God, please God, please make it stop.*

Steve clawed at the last of the wrapping paper round the painting as a machine gun on the tank spat flame and bullets across the compound, shattering the bottles in the pool bar just like Karen had seen in old Westerns on the telly. From behind the tanks leapt small groups of men, firing indiscriminately and shouting in Spanish as they fanned out around the pool. The British group hugged the side of the wall, curling themselves into balls.

Ian screamed and lunged at Steve. 'That painting's worth four million pounds, if it gets damaged my career will be ruined!'

Steve gave a parade ground roar that would have been enough to shatter every window in a barracks.

'I don't care about your career, or this crap!'

With a dull crack, he punched Ian on the jaw. The smaller man dropped to the ground, clutching his face, as Steve leapt forward onto the edge of the pool and brandished the painting in the air above his head, turning from left to right.

There was excited shouting from the rubble on the other side of the pool and the ragged looking men stopped firing, watching Steve warily. A small bearded man with a rusty rifle gabbled excitedly through a hatch on the side of the tank and pointed at Steve. Second later the tank roared into reverse gear in a cloud of exhaust fumes, and backed onto the drive with the revolutionaries following on foot.

Karen screamed with relief. 'Oh my God it's worked, oh Steve, it's worked!'

The rest of the group started chattering excitedly, except for Ian, who lay on the ground groaning and rubbing his jaw.

Steve whooped and shouted with delight. 'Bloody hell, how's that for a result?'

He turned away from the armed men, still holding the painting aloft. Steve pointed out over the compound wall and shouted.

'The other lot are on the run now, look!'

Karen heard a sharp crack and a whine, then looked in horror as Steve's head jerked back, a spurt of blood jetting from his jaw. His body pirouetted off the edge of the pool and fell forwards with a sickening crash into a heap on a plastic sun lounger.

Karen rushed forward. 'Steve, Steve.' She looked around wildly. 'Quick, somebody help him.'

Angie looked dazed. 'I thought they'd stopped shooting?' She said it as if she was talking about it stopping raining.

'No, it wasn't that lot that came in, it was the other lot out there,' said Pauline. 'The government lot, or whatever they are. Look, they're running away now.'

The group gathered round Steve and Pauline moved to lift him forward. Trisha looked alarmed.

'You're not supposed to move them,' she said.

Please don't let him be dead, thought Karen. *Steve, I'm sorry, I didn't mean anything I said to you.*

'You can move them if it's more dangerous to leave them be,' said Pauline. 'Put pressure on the wound, that's what you're supposed to do'.

Pauline had taken charge, bustling with her new found confidence as Angie looked on with a blank expression. 'I did one of them St John's courses at work,' she explained.

She grabbed a towel and lifted Steve up. His face was deathly white, and blood poured down his shirt and over the painting, still clutched in his hand.

Pauline said loudly 'Steve, can you hear me, open your eyes!' There was no response.

Karen saw the hard concrete of the poolside rush up towards her, just as everything went black.

****

Ian's jaw felt like it had swollen to twice its normal size, and he winced as he rubbed it and moved it from side to side. *At least it can't be broken then*, he thought, and there didn't seem to be anything wrong with his teeth. He'd never been in a fight before, much less ever been punched in the face, but he'd no idea it would ever hurt this much.

He shook his head and sat up. He was still a bit dazed and hadn't managed to quite take in what had happened with Steve. Had he been shot? *Serve the stupid prat right,* he thought. *I had the situation under control.* Now it looked like Karen had collapsed as well.

'It's alright, she's only fainted' he heard Trisha say, and he saw the blowsy woman help Karen to her feet and put her in a chair.

At least the shooting had stopped so he got up, wincing with pain, and walked over to see what had happened. Suddenly he remembered. *The painting!* He raced over to the lounger on which Steve was lying, skidding over the debris of masonry and broken bottles, and pushed through the small group like a rubbernecker at a road accident.

'Is everything ok?' he asked eagerly.

Pauline looked up from nursing Steve. His eyes flickered. 'He's alright. The bleeding's stopped, it must have just been a graze on his ear. They bleed a lot, the ears. I think the bullet just missed him, thank God.'

'No, I mean the painting,' blurted out Ian.

Ignoring the glare from Karen, Ian looked down at Steve's midriff and was horrified to see a hole ripped in the canvas, and a large smear of brownish blood streaked across it.

'Oh my god the painting!' he yelled.

He grabbed it and held it up to the dim glow from the hotel's emergency lighting, the last of the daylight now gone. Feverishly he rubbed at the blood with his jacket sleeve – *sod Oswald Boateng,* he thought, *this is worth two thousand of his elitist jackets.* It only made the stain worse.

Ian felt cold rush of horror creep across his body, and swallowed hard as he realised what had happened. He slumped into a padded plastic chair, which made a farting noise as the cushion split under the impact. Ian vaguely wondered if anyone would think he'd actually farted.

'It…it's ruined.' He cradled the painting gently, like a sleeping child.

Karen stood up and screamed at him. 'It's only a bloody painting, for Christ's bloody sake!'

Then she collapsed in her chair, sobbing. *Nerves,* thought Ian. *She doesn't know what she's saying.*

'It's a modern masterpiece,' said Ian, slowly. 'And I was supposed to be looking after it. Just look at it – it's ruined. *I'm* ruined – I'll be the laughing stock of the art world.'

Steve chuckled and sat up, wincing as he took the bloodstained towel from Pauline and held it to his earlobe.

'Look mate...'

'He's alright, he's woken up now,' she said with relief.

Karen grabbed Steve and held him close. 'Thank God you're alright,' she sobbed, and held his face in her hands as she kissed him. He winced as her hand pressed too hard on the towel.

'Sorry about the painting,' croaked Steve.

Karen hissed. 'Don't you *dare* say you're sorry to him.'

Pauline tried to conciliate. 'Don't excite yourself, love,' she said to Karen, who brushed her aside and sniffed back tears.

'No – let me speak. Steve could have been killed but he stopped us being shot at without a thought for himself. He's lucky to be alive and all you can worry about is your poxy painting. Well I think that's disgusting.'

Angie had miraculously found some cigarettes somewhere and lit up, breathing an angry plume of smoke at Ian, who coughed slightly. The smoke seemed to revive her slightly.

'She's right. You should be ashamed of yourself. Anyway, it's bound to be insured, in't it?'

Ian was dumbstruck. *What is wrong with these people?* he thought, looking around at their hostile eyes.

'Insured…that's not important! It's worth more than just…just money!'

Steve chuckled again. He seemed much better now.

'Look mate, I know it's supposed to be great work of art and all that, but come on, look at it. A quick clean and repair and that'll be good as new.'

Angie snorted and flicked ash in the general direction of the painting. 'You could even paint a new one and nobody would know the difference.'

Everyone except Ian burst out laughing, Angie's chuckling descending into hacking coughs. *It must be some sort of post traumatic stress*, thought Ian. *They're probably going to need counselling.* For a moment he wondered if he could get away with having it mended, then dismissed the thought with disgust.

'Don't be ridiculous. The experts would spot all that straight away. No, I'm just going to have to face the music. Well that's it. The end of my career.' He slumped back in his seat and pulled his iphone out of his pocket, only to find that the gadget's screen was shattered and it wouldn't turn on.

Karen was still quivering with anger. 'Aren't you forgetting something? Steve just risked his life for you. If it wasn't for him it might have been the end of your life, not just your career. Aren't you even grateful? To think I *admired* you because you were clever, and knew about art. Well you can keep all that.'

There was an embarrased pause. *Has she just admitted she fancied me?* It made him think of Jenny, waiting at home, not knowing anything about all this; perhaps he might have had the chance of an affair with a stranger behind her back. He realised that when he got home, he would put off something he'd been meaning to do for ages. He would finally pluck up the courage to suggest they have an open relationship.

He drew a deep breath and decided perhaps a little bit of humble pie wouldn't go amiss.

'Well…look….I'm sorry. Look it's all been a bit…emotional today. You're right. It is only a painting after all. It'll be tough breaking the news to Miguel, but maybe it can be mended. Steve, you did a great job, and I owe you one, mate. I'm sorry for what I said before.'

He offered a hand to Steve who shook it firmly.

'Don't worry about it,' said Steve. 'People do funny things under fire. And I'm sorry I had to smack you, even though you deserved it. We're all alright, that's the main thing.'

Ian smiled. 'Yes. And Karen, I owe you an apology too.' As he looked at her sullen face he realised he didn't really fancy her much after all. He genuinely meant to be apologetic.

Karen sniffed. 'Look, just forget about it. Like you said, it's all been a bit of a shock.'

'I'm not surprised we're all a bit shaken up,' sighed Pauline. 'You don't get shot at every day of the week do you?'

Angie jabbed a finger at Ian. 'He's from London. They're used to it down there.'

Steve got up slowly, clutching the lounger for support. 'Well I think we could all do with a drink. Why don't we see if any bottles are left standing at the bar?'

There was enthusiastic agreement and everyone moved towards the ruins of the pool bar. Ian was anxious to get the story out to the media, but with a busted phone, there was very little he could do. He realised it would just have to wait until they got to the Embassy.

He'd always fancied himself as a foreign correspondent, and previously he'd thought that if it all blew up in San Itairi, perhaps he could pull strings to get back on the BBC, giving calm and collected reports on the conflict while wearing a blue helmet and bullet proof vest, the camera focusing on a discarded child's shoe in a heap of rubble... Now, that idea didn't seem quite so glamorous, and a stiff drink a far better alternative.

Everybody turned as they heard the roar of an engine beyond the ruins of the reception area. A large limousine pulled up, smeared with dust and with the revolutionary flag trailing from the passenger window like a football scarf. A cortege of equally dusty luxury cars and limousines lined up behind. A figure in camouflage clothing toting a gleaming machine gun stepped out of the first limo, and Ian caught a whiff of cigar smoke as the man strode towards them, flanked by armed guards.

It was Miguel. Ian dashed forward excitedly, hoping to finally get some news of the revolution. Then he remembered. *The painting!*

Thirteen

Before Ian had time to think of what to say, Miguel clasped him in a bear hug, definitely too close for comfort, and kissed him on both cheeks. The man stank of body odour and cigars, though Ian reflected he probably wasn't too fragrant himself. The armed guards gazed on impassively as Miguel draped his arm around Ian and began walking with him towards the huddled group by the shattered bar, who had managed to find an unharmed bottle of rum which they were passing round eagerly.

'Ian, you are safe! I was so worried, that those fascist pigs could have injured you. I am so sorry that these lapdogs of the imperialist American swine should have upset you. Worry no more – we have driven those *hijos de putans* into the sea. The battle is over!'

Angie grimaced. 'Who on earth's that? He's not one of that lot that blew the place up is he?'

Ian looked around sheepishly. Although he was glad to hear the revolution had succeeded, he realised he was going to have to handle the matter of the painting very delicately.

'Er…everybody…this is Miguel Corantes, the conceptual artist. The one I came here to interview.'

Miguel laughed and shrugged his shoulders. 'Artist…pah – a bourgeois title.'

'Oh, er…sorry…'

'Ian, I consider myself more a craftsman. A *builder.*'

'Well if you're a builder, you should start getting this place cleaned up,' said Angie.

Miguel stepped forward and took Angie's hand. To her surprise he lifted it to his lips and kissed it. A blush spread over her jowls. He did the same to Trisha, Pauline and Karen.

'*Senoras*…my English, she is not so good…*Como se diace in Ingles?* I do not mean a builder of houses, but a builder of dreams and visions. That is the true work of the artist.'

'Look love, we've no idea what you're on about,' said Pauline.

Karen's face lit up. 'Don't you realise who he is? He's the one who painted the flag.'

Miguel grinned and raised his arms. 'Ah, I see, a woman who appreciates and understands art. So rare in your country. And who is this?' He looked admiringly at Steve.

'This is my boyfriend, Steve.'

'*Encantado!*' Miguel moved to kiss Steve on the cheeks but he stepped back sharply.

Steve looked at Miguel. 'Hang on, so you did that painting...listen, we had a bit of a...'

Ian bustled forward and led Miguel to one side. 'It's alright Miguel, let's go over to the bar shall we, and have a drink? I'm sure we could all do with one...'

Miguel didn't move. 'Yes, yes of course, but first...I must get what I came for. I must regain *Deliverance*'.

This was the moment Ian had been dreading. To his surprise, he'd felt pretty calm during the fire-fight, but the thought of what Miguel might do to him when he saw what had happened to his property filled him with dread. He'd never had to cope with anything like this in his career to date. Upsetting a few reactionaries on radio panel discussions was one thing, but ruining the most valuable artwork of a heavily armed artistic genius was another. He looked warily at Miguel and saw a zealous gleam in his eyes.

'Only now has my vision achieved reality. Only now can the flag of the people of San Itairi regain its rightful place in our palace of justice in the capital. Quickly, Ian, bring the painting to me.'

Ian felt his voice go up a notch again and he swallowed hard to get it back down to normal. He noticed the rest of the group had gone quiet and were watching him closely.

'Ah...er, there's a slight problem I'm afraid.'

'Problem…you do still have the painting?'

'Ah…yes.'

'Good, good. Then quickly, bring it to me. The crowds are already starting to gather in the main square. The people are demanding to see the painting, and I must show it to them.'

'Ah….'

Ian's mouth was beginning to open and close like a goldfish as he tried desperately to think of something to say. Then Steve came forward. Ian wasn't sure if this was a good thing; on one hand at least it would show it wasn't his fault that the painting had been ruined; but on the other, Steve wasn't likely to be tactful when it came to dealing with the artistic temperament.

Steve clapped Ian on the shoulder with alarming force. 'Listen, I'll tell him. It was my idea anyway.' He turned to Miguel.

'Look mate, I'm sorry, but your painting got a bit damaged, in all the confusion with the shooting and that.'

Miguel's face took on a look of grave concern. 'Damaged? How damaged? *You must show me!'*

Steve led the way to the side of the pool and the group followed closely behind. He picked up the damaged canvas from where someone had propped it on a lounger and handed it to Miguel.

Ian gave a hysterical laugh. 'Listen, Miguel, I can explain...'

Miguel's fat fingers prodded and probed the damage to the canvas. His eyes widened in alarm.

'Questo? Que pasar? What, what is this? Holes, blood...what has happened to the painting?'

Ian slumped into a poolside chair. He put his head in his hands. *Oh God, there goes my career,* he thought again. He dimly wondered if he could be held financially responsible for it in some way as well.

Karen took a deep breath and stepped forward to stand next to Steve.

'I'm sorry, but Steve had to show the painting to your men in the tanks. It was the only way to stop them shooting, and they did, but the other lot, the soldiers who ran away, shot at him instead. That's why it's got bullet holes and blood on it. We didn't know what else to do.'

There was a long pause and then a huge grin spread across Miguel's face. Ian looked at him closely, wondering if the man was about to flip his lid and start shooting.

'This…this is incredible! You mean to tell me, that this young English man raised this painting, and for that…for *that*, was shot by the fascist jackals of the reactionary government?' Miguel's eyes flicked up to the congealing blood on the side of Steve's head.

'But wait, you are wounded – you are not badly hurt…?'

Steve grinned and put his arm round Karen's waist. 'I'll live.'

Ian wondered if he might just have managed to get away with it. Miguel didn't seem to be taking it too badly – in fact he seemed to be taking it quite well. He touched Miguel on the arm.

'Look, I know a very good art restorer at Tate Modern, he can…'

Miguel screwed up his eyes and raised his voice. 'No, no no *no!*'

Ian jumped back involuntarily. Angie looked at Pauline and raised her eyebrows. 'Oh blimey, he's not happy,' she whispered. 'They get emotional, these artists.'

Pauline, who had been watching intently, waved Angie away. 'Shh, Ange you'll only make things worse'.

Miguel raised the painting to the sky, a look of exaltation on his face. 'This is the *best* thing that ever could have happened!'

Ian's brain whirled in confusion. 'What…?'

Miguel stabbed his finger into the holes in the canvas. 'Look – this painting, symbol of the hopes and aspirations of the San Itarian people for decades…stained with the blood of an English martyr fighting for freedom. The people will rejoice!'

Steve laughed. 'I wasn't fighting for freedom, mate. It was just a graze.'

Miguel smiled. 'Ah, ah, the famous English understatement, my man you are a true martyr for the cause of freedom, like, like, your Lord Byron!'

Steve looked blank and Angie leant over to him to explain. 'Byron. He invented the ballpoint pen.'

Miguel ignored this and clasped Steve by the hand. 'My friend, if there is anything I can do for you – *anything* – just tell me'.

Steve drew Miguel closer. 'Well, there is something...' He whispered into Miguel's ear. Miguel grinned and nodded his head furiously.

'Of course my friend, of course, it will be just as you wish!'

Ian wondered what all that was about. He noticed Karen was looking puzzled too. He decided he hadn't the energy left to care. What was important was that it looked like he might have managed to pull off the greatest comeback since Frank Sinatra. He smiled tentatively at Miguel. It was still best to be cautious, he thought.

'You mean you think the painting's been *improved?* But the monetary value…'

Miguel scoffed and for a moment Ian wondered if he'd gone too far. He soon realised however that he *had* managed to pull it off. Miguel set the painting down on a chair and grasped Ian's shoulders.

'You talk of money? How can a value be put on this? I am a user of mere paint. But this man, he use his *blood*. If anything, it will be worth more. It will be worth double.'

'Really? Well, of course, I can see that it does give it interesting provenance.'

This time it was Karen's turn to look confused. 'What's provenance?' she asked Ian.

Angie leant in again to explain. 'It's a place in the south of France where posh people go on holiday.'

Ian was oblivious to the chatter around him as Miguel shook his shoulders.

'Ian – I need you by my side. I need you to tell this story to the world. Tell them of how the blood of freedom was spilled on the canvas of true art. You must telephone to your newspaper straight away.'

'Er…yes, of course. Of course I knew you'd understand Miguel.'

It suddenly occurred to him that Miguel was right. This could be big – really big. And he wouldn't have to fanny around with a blue helmet and a flak jacket either. Of course, that was fine, the guys who did that did a great job, but perhaps that was best left to the professionals like Jeremy Bowen. *No*, decided Ian. His place was in London – telling the world what was happening in San Itairi through the medium of art and cultural commentary. There might even be a book deal in it, and they'd *have* to let him on *Newsnight*. He started to imagine himself in the green room at the BBC, chatting and swapping stories with Paxman or maybe even Dimbleby.

He was woken from his daydream by the sound of Steve pushing his chair back and quickly getting up.

'Well you can leave us out of it. I just want to get back home.'

There were murmurs of agreement from Karen, Angie, Pauline, and Trisha. Miguel, however, suddenly looked concerned.

'Home – you mean to England? My friends, this is not possible. The airport is badly damaged from bombing in the coup – it will be at least a week before it is repaired. We are putting the tourists in tents by the airport.'

Angie looked downcast and said slowly 'you mean we have to stay in a tent for a week?'

Ian expected her to start mouthing off again but instead she just looked down at the ground and bit her lip.

Miguel laughed again. 'My friends – there is no need to stay here. You can stay with me.'

Pauline and Karen murmured approvingly and even Angie perked up a bit.

Ian suddenly remembered that Miguel had made a move on him. He swallowed nervously.

'But you've only got one room in your studio. We couldn't all fit in there.'

Miguel beamed as he led the way 'Ah, my friends, in all the excitement I forgot to tell you. I have just come from the Palace of Justice, where the revolutionary government unanimously elected me as…Minister of Culture!'

Pauline looked worried. 'That sounds nice love, but it don't solve our accommodation problems.'

Miguel lit a huge cigar, blowing clouds of smoke into the air, and smiled. 'Ah, but it does. You will all be my guests at the Presidential Palace. For as long as you wish!'

****

Pauline was exhausted, too tired to notice the plush, leather lined interior of the limousine that she, Angie and Trisha were sitting in. They had the huge car to themselves as the cortege began its slow journey to the Presidential Palace. She looked over at Angie with a worried expression. She'd been very quiet, and was staring out at the rubble strewn streets, or the little of what could be seen of them in the light from the few streetlamps that were working. *Any minute now she'll start complaining*, she thought. She wondered if she would lose it completely if Angie said one more word of complaint, especially in front of this girl that had done her best in a difficult situation and looked about ready to collapse.

'Paul...' said Angie, turning to look at Pauline.

Here it comes, thought Pauline, clenching her fists.

Angie spoke slowly, fixing her eyes on the back of the driver's head.

'All that time we were in there, when the bullets were flying, and we were crouched up against that wall, I couldn't help noticing, it hadn't had a lick of paint in God knows how long.'

Pauline felt hysterical laughter rising up inside her. Angie, however, gripped Pauline's hand and looked at her closely.

'I mean, we could have died back there, and all I could bloody think about was some silly paint.'

'Are you feeling alright, Ange...?'

'I've never felt better. And I thought to myself, mam's parents got killed in Coventry in the Blitz when she were just a girl. Our dad nearly got killed on D-Day as well, and he were only 19.'

'Well, what's that got to do with owt?' She wondered if Angie had really lost it.

Angie smiled again. Pauline realised she'd hardly ever seen her smile. It took years off her.

'I mean, they never complained about anything. On holiday, mam and dad. Never once. In all the years we went on holiday in all sort of mucky places like Blackpool or Skegness, they never said a word, even though they could have done. I used to think it was daft, and that you should speak up. I'm not so sure it matters now. I think I can see why they were like that. They were probably just glad to be alive.'

Pauline sighed with relief. *Maybe next year's holiday won't be so bad*, she thought. *Well, it could hardly be worse than this one.*

She looked over at Trisha who had been listening intently to their conversation.

'I have to say, ladies, at this time, that I really admire what you just said. In fact, I've been doing a bit of thinking to myself, myself, and I think you're dead right. About being happy to be alive, that is. You were spot on about that hotel, it was a load of rubbish and I've had enough of it.'

'You were only doing your job love, and you did it well,' said Angie. Pauline wondered if she'd had some sort of religious conversion. Trisha looked adamant. She took out a compact and began heavily powdering her face.

'No, I was living a false lie that wasn't true. I've decided I'm going to leave San Itairi and I'm going to start my own hotel somewhere civilised and English.'

'That sounds nice love,' said Pauline. 'Whereabouts will you go?'

'I thought perhaps Corfu.'

Pauline smiled. 'That sounds lovely. We might even visit you next year.'

'Look, Paul, look!' said Angie. 'This is must be where we're staying!'

Angie was pointing like an excited child out of the passenger window. Pauline's jaw dropped as the limousine pulled up outside what she realised must be the Presidential Palace. It was an immense, immaculate white floodlit building with balconies and shutters all over the place, like something you'd see on the telly about Monte Carlo. A fountain surrounded by palm trees gushed in the centre of a gravelled carriage turn as the limousine crunched to a halt. A ragged man with a rifle slung across his back leapt forward to open the car door, clicking his heels smartly as Trisha stepped out.

Pauline suddenly remembered there was a way you were supposed to get out of a limousine, like the Royals did, but she couldn't remember how, and anyway, she decided that might only be for sports cars. So she stepped out as in as dignified a way as she could. Angie clutched at her for support as she followed.

'Just look at this place,' said Pauline, staring at the marbled steps leading up to the giant double doors.

Angie smiled and winked at her as the armed man dragged their cases from the boot.

'Do you think there'll be bingo?'

They both cracked up laughing.

****

As Pauline, Angie and Trisha were shown to their rooms, Miguel ushered Ian out of the limousine and into the main lobby of the Palace. Ian was a little troubled by the ostentatious display of the car.

'Isn't this all a bit...I mean, what happened to that old car you had?'

'You forget I am now a government minister, Ian. That small car would not have been suitable.'

'Well…I thought in your work you always disliked the trappings of the bourgeoisie? Didn't you once say you drove a small car because you were a man of the people?'

Miguel chuckled as he led the way up a thickly carpeted double staircase.

'Ian, Ian, you British…you have a lot to learn about politics. I am a man of the people, yes – but the people, they *expect* a government minister to drive a limousine. So, I am giving them what they want.'

Ian still wasn't sure about this as Miguel showed him into the largest bedroom he'd ever seen. Miguel was speaking like a tour guide as he rapidly opened cupboard doors and demonstrated how the lights worked.

'I must go soon to show *Deliverance* to the people. But you may make yourself at home here. The palace has everything you will need – a private beach, a state banqueting hall, a huge wine cellar…'

Ian felt a warm glow as he looked at the four poster bed and chandeliers, the room full of the kind of furniture that he usually hated, the antique sort you saw in stately homes. He had to admit, however, that it had a certain charm and it was definitely an improvement on the Las Cantatas hotel.

'This was the President's bedroom,' announced Miguel with pride.

Ian's heart skipped a beat. He was going to be writing the official story of the San Itairian uprising from the actual bedroom of the deposed President. His thoughts raced. Who else had ever done that? Wasn't there some photographer who'd stayed in Hitler's bedroom after he'd been killed? He'd have to brush up on all this for his book. Then he stopped.

'But...what's happened to the President? Where will he stay before his trial?'

The man might be a fascist, but all the same, Ian felt an innate middle-class English guilt at barging into someone's private quarters, apparently without permission.

Miguel laughed, and Ian noticed the look of fervour that he'd seen once or twice before.

'Ian, you are so naive. Firstly, this did not belong to the President. He only robbed this from the people of San Itairi. So we are only taking back what is rightfully ours.'

Ian nodded to himself. Of course, Miguel was right. *All property is theft.* He hadn't felt this good since he was a teenager, when he'd tried to get a flight to China after the Tiananmen Square uprising had started. His parents had refused to lend him the money, but the sense of wanting to be part of a revolution had never left him.

'And secondly, there will be no trial of the President.'

Ian swallowed. The warm, luxurious feeling he'd had on seeing the room was starting to dissipate.

'No...trial?'

'What need for one? I killed him myself, in this very room.'

'Ah.'

'But don't worry, there was no blood, so nothing has been spoilt.'

Ian felt a cold horror creep up his spine. 'No...blood?'

'No, I strangled him. These hands, Ian...they can create, but if necessary, they can also destroy.'

Ian suddenly felt an urgent need to go to the lavatory, and looked hopefully at a door in the corner.

'Is that the loo?' he squeaked.

Miguel looked puzzled. 'No, that is another bedroom. It is superstition I know, but somehow I would feel wrong about sleeping in the same room in which I killed a man, however evil he was. So I will be right next door to you, Ian. We will have so much to talk about, as you write the story of my life. What will you call it? *My Destiny?* No, I have a better idea. *My Struggle.*'

Ian thought vaguely that the title might have been used before, but he couldn't remember where. Miguel steered him out of the room and down the main stairs where the limousine was waiting.

'Come, Ian, the crowds are waiting to see *Deliverance*, and I must show it to them. Now, you must rest. It will take a long, long time to write my story. Perhaps months.'

'Months...erm, but...'

Miguel waved his objections away and took out a set of large keys. 'Ian, you are a great writer, perhaps it will only take weeks. But it must be done. Now I must go. Please do not be alarmed, but I must lock the door, for your own safety. There still may be agents loyal to the President around, and your life could be at risk. So, now, rest, and when I return, we will liberate the very good Bollinger that is in the cellar. We will discuss the future of socialism – over a glass of champagne!'

Before Ian could protest, Miguel had disappeared through the door, and he heard a rattle as the key turned in the lock. Ian swallowed again, wondering if this revolution business was all it was cracked up to be.

He suddenly felt a long, long way from north London.

****

Karen was still not sure what was going on. Steve had put her in one of the limousines but had told her to wait there for a few minutes as he had to go and sort something out. She'd watched as the other two limos had departed but their car had just sat there in the dark, and Steve was nowhere to be seen. She'd tried to speak to the shabbily dressed driver through the dividing window, but he'd just shrugged his shoulders and said something that must have meant he didn't understand English.

She'd thought about the events of the afternoon. When all the shooting had been going on, she'd realised she loved Steve more than anything. All the silly squabbles about books and art and paintings and whether he wore shorts or jeans seemed so pointless. That scene with Ian had clinched it for her. If that was 'culture' you could keep it – the man might have seemed glamorous at first but he'd shown he was really just a pompous, posh dickhead and Steve was worth ten of him.

After what seemed like an eternity but was probably only about 20 minutes, she breathed a sigh of relief as Steve opened the door of the car.

'Thank God, you're back, what's going on? The others have all left.'

Steve smiled. 'Come on, this way.'

He helped her out of the low car and they walked across the heap of rubble that had been the reception area. The heavily damaged hotel looked almost like some sort of romantic ruin in the moonlight, with the dim emergency lighting reflected on the calm water of the deserted swimming pool.

Karen was exhausted and in no mood for games. 'Steve, what's going on? I've had just about as many surprises as I can stand today. I just want to go to bed.'

Steve ignored her. 'Nearly there now.'

Karen realised they had come to the accommodation block where she'd spied on him earlier. Most of the building was undamaged but a rocket or something must have hit the roof, as it had completely disappeared and the building lay open to the stars.

Steve took Karen's hand and led her up the concrete steps to the upper floor. 'Sorry about the wait, I had to check it was all safe. The roof's gone but the rest's ok.'

He opened the door to the room where she'd seen him with whats-her-name, Anna. What on earth was going on? Her tired brain reeled. Wildly she wondered if Steve was trying to set up some sort of threesome with this other woman. Surely not, he'd never seemed that type. So then what was he planning?

Suddenly she noticed that in the middle of the room was not a bed but a large table, laid with a white cloth and fancy plates much nicer than the ones in the dining room. There was even one of those metal buckets with a bottle of champagne and a napkin in it.

'It's all still here, thank God.' Steve blew some dust off the table and wiped the champagne bottle. He struggled with the cork.

'Always looks easy on the telly, doesn't it?' He smiled. There was a pop and the wine fizzed from the bottle. Steve quickly poured it into two glasses and handed one to Karen.

'Cheers'.

They clinked glasses and Karen took a swig, relishing the taste. She'd forgotten how thirsty she was and the champagne, despite being warm, was refreshing. She wondered if Steve had somehow gone funny after the shock of being shot, but he looked perfectly calm, and his head wound looked barely noticeable now.

Steve cleared his throat. 'Before you say anything, I know you think I've been an idiot and I know I should have explained everything, but I never got the chance with what's been going on. This was supposed to be a proper posh dinner for us. I got this girl from the hotel who does parties and that, Anna she's called, to sort it all out but as you can see it got a bit disrupted. I knew it was going to cost a bomb, I just didn't know we'd actually *get* bombed.'

So that was the mysterious Anna. Karen still had countless questions to ask. 'But why....'

'Shh. It's because I want to ask you something. I'm not much good at romantic stuff so I thought I'd do it all proper, but the whole thing's got ballsed up now what with me being shot and everything. So anyway, I'll stop going on, and just ask you one thing.'

Karen felt a rush of adrenaline as she realised what he was about to do. He went down on one knee and they both laughed as he brushed debris out of the way, then he took a small box from his shorts pocket and gave it to her.

'So what I'm asking is, will you marry me?'

Karen didn't register the question until she opened the little velvet box to reveal a tiny, perfect diamond on a Tiffany-style setting, glittering in the moonlight which shone through the shattered roof of the hotel room. Suddenly she realised what was happening.

'No...no....no!' she gasped, breathlessly, and clutched her hand to her mouth.

Steve looked crestfallen. 'No?'

Karen corrected herself. 'No, I mean, no I don't believe it. I mean yes, yes of course!'

She threw her arms around him and they kissed. Karen decided she didn't ever want to let Steve's arms be unwrapped from her, but after some time he disentangled himself and led her out of the ruined room.

'Come on babes. We'd best get back to the car, I've no idea how long the driver will hang around.'

Karen laughed. 'We came in a bus and left in a limo. This holiday has certainly turned out to be a bit different.'

'You can say that again. You'll have a few stories to tell the people on your art course.'

'I thought you didn't like me going on that course?'

Steve paused as they reached the pool area and picked up their cases, reassured that the car was still waiting for them. He waved at the driver then turned to Karen.

'No, don't be stupid. I don't mind. I might even come along. After all, I'm an artist myself now aren't I?'

Karen looked puzzled but then Steve pointed to the wound on the side of his head as they strolled towards the car.

'I suppose you are,' laughed Karen. 'Though paint's usually a bit easier to use than blood.'

Steve chuckled as he held open the door to the limo. 'Just wait 'til I tell them about all this down the pub. They'll think I'm a right ponce!'

Karen sighed as she thought of their dull local pub on a wet, windy English evening. Then she felt Steve squeeze her hand reassuringly, and suddenly, she couldn't wait to get back there.

Other books by Hugh Morrison

The Dalai Lama Next Door
The Slow Bicycle Companion
The Frugal Gentleman

Printed in Great Britain
by Amazon.co.uk, Ltd.,
Marston Gate.